THE GREENHOUSE

How We Grow, Book 2

SONYA YOUNG

Edited by
CAROL WILLIAMS

Illustrated by
BOBBY BARNHILL

LAKEVIEW
PUBLICATIONS

CONTENTS

Printed in the United States of America

First Printing, 2021

ISBN: 978-0-578-25314-5

Book Cover Design: Bobby Barnhill
Editing: Carol Williams
Formatting: Craig A. Price
Publisher: LakeView Publications

For future generations to come. For my children I've yet to meet and for the grace that follows life after life.

GRATITUDE

I am grateful for the scientists: the silent warriors in the background who stand watch over our planet, awaiting the next spark of brilliance to fuel their creativity.

I am grateful for the apiculturists who are literally saving our lives with every breath they breathe into a new hive. I am eternally grateful for your tenderness toward these sacred creatures.

I am grateful for the farmers, closest to the earth, the voice of the soil, for your tireless dedication with every crop, never knowing the outcome until you harvest. You are the risk-takers and the dreamers and the nurturers to us all. Thank You.

Finally, to the explorers and the seekers. It is your fascination, curiosity, and willingness to go beyond yourself which guarantees our very existence. I am grateful for your courage and your fearlessness in the face of the Unknown.

I stood under a tree today.
I stood under a tree today and unleashed grief disappointment
and unmet expectations.
Sadness too powerful to articulate exited my body through a
primal howl of pain anger and tears.
Absorbing it all, the earth fractured sending multiple
aftershocks through and below me. With each new fissure the
pain anger and frustration flowed out of me like water exiting
my feet entering the ground.
I gather blankets pillows and earplugs to swaddle myself in layer
after layer of protection.
So, I do not have to see.
And I do not have to hear.
And I do not have to feel.
I lay down and press myself into the earth unwilling to
acknowledge the role I played.
I stood under a tree today and collapsed into it.

PROLOGUE

Over time, Mehlin's tears became part of the soil, like nature's fertilizer, along with the sadness and longing. As if the earth received each tear and recognized Mehlin's unyielding love for Reya, returning his gratitude and appreciation with dark nutrient-rich land. Each visit, each step he walked over the years felt by the earth and the Unknown. Until finally, Mehlin, too, returned to the soil. The fertile land regenerated, regained its strength, and began again. Deep below the cracks and the running water fed by time, love, and mystery, are the seeds that Reya buried years ago. Like precious cocoons wrapped in the wisdom of the Unknown, they were not yet ready to ascend. The seeds were waiting, sensing, and listening for the right Moment to awaken. Awaken a space, awaken a spirit, and possibly awaken a heart.

IN THE DISTANCE THE MOUNTAINS REMAINED VIGILANT. THEY REMEMBER THE ESSENCE THAT ONCE FILLED THE MEADOW AND HOW HER PRESENCE ROUSED A CURIOSITY AND PLAY IN THEM.

THERE WERE TALKS AMONG THEM ABOUT LEAVING. VIIME WAS BORED AND WANTED TO EXPLORE. TULEVAISUUS FELT DRAWN BY WHAT HE SENSED WERE OTHER GIANTS. STILL, THEY REMAINED: WATCHING, SENSING, AND LISTENING FOR SOMETHING FRESH AND NEW TO HEIGHTEN THEIR INTEREST.

Beyond the meadow, the forest is alive and thriving. Veli along with his children born from his own roots are showing promise. Their tender leaves exude freshness and flexibility to move and sway with each breeze that blows into the forest. Still sparse in areas, indications of life returning are visible with the reappearance of rabbits, squirrels and butterflies. Humming in the center of it all are the rocks that maintain the circle that surrounded Aiti. A heartbeat emanates from them, pulsating silent sonnets to awaken the earth and the sky. The waves of love flowing out so delicately that only the most sensitive can feel them and thus answer their call.

Meanwhile, Nea watches her son sway in his playpen as if dancing to a silent song that only he can hear. He is a beautiful, tender baby who is happiest when he sits next to her in the garden, playing with flowers and worms and bugs. He holds the dirt and squishes it between his tiny fingers and giggles. Giggles that melt Nea's heart. Giggles felt by the Unknown who in turn begins a playfulness with Terve.

CHAPTER 1
SOMEWHERE ELSE

G lass walls framed with cedar and copper accents. Strategically placed vertical copper and wooden beams along with alternating bamboo plants give the illusion of blinds. The floor, slightly lower than the rest of the bathroom, is completely made from cedar planks while the ceiling is exactly like the walls. A Japanese maple's branches slightly creep over the ceiling. Extending downward is an oversized square rain showerhead. Because the head extends from the ceiling, it truly feels like outside, showering in the rain. The wide-open shower has no door, and the walls are only concealed by nature.

The water turned on full blast and as hot as he can stand it, he steps in and places his large, calloused hands shoulder-width apart and leans into the shower. His grey hair with sandy brown highlights flattens out under the weight of the water pounding his head and shoulders. He rounds his back slightly and lowers his head even more, so his shoulder muscles feel the full force of the water. Responding slowly, his muscles release as the hot water covers them like a warm blanket. His shoulders, like the rest of his body, exude strength and discipline; the kind of strength that is earned through hard work and conviction. His body is a testament to what he loves and nurtures. Standing slightly over six feet, he exhales loudly. Finally, he can breathe fully without strain in his neck and back. Feeling better, he looks at the tree above. A squirrel scampers across the ceiling, taking a second to pause and look down at the man. He scrubs his defined muscles with a brush and bar soap made from goat's milk. Milk from his goats. Scrubbing and stretching, he is grateful for this amazing shower. He likes feeling open and vulnerable to nature. He has spent his entire life farming here.

The goat's milk cleanses his skin but also rejuvenates it with moisture and vitamins. Setting the brush down, Terve lathers up again, using his hands this time. As he passes over his body, symbols flicker in the sunlight. Symbols he's acquired over the years. They show up covertly and without warning. Sometimes, they appear subdued while other times they remain visible on his skin like his other tattoos. They have been with him so many years now, he often forgets they are there. He believes they like the water or the soap because they always flicker while in the shower. Perhaps they are just awakening with his touch. Finishing up, he looks up one last time before he turns off the water and surrenders to the fact that he must get ready for the day.

The rest of the bathroom follows his rustic essence. The floating vanity is from a massive piece of black walnut. It looks like it was from a ship or a very old building. Mammoth nails remain in the piece which acts as anchor for the two towel hooks that he installed. The sink, a Tibetan-looking bowl, floats atop the walnut with a copper faucet placed just inside the rim. At first glance, it looks like an old pump system instead of modern plumbing. The only colors in the room are provided by nature: copper accented with greens from oxidation, and the cedarwood's fiery red grains alongside the rich deep brown-black color of the walnut, towels and washcloths the color of oatmeal, rust surrounding the nails and the floor mats the color of earth.

The room fills him with the Earth and its glorious pallet of colors.

He stands in front of the modest mirror that hangs over the sink and talks to himself about his day. Hazel eyes with a gold ring stare back at him. Lips open and full, his teeth glisten just behind. His hair drying off is jagged at the edges and symmetrically hanging from his head. With each flick of the brush, he feels air breathe into him messages of love and kindness. He enjoys the kind words and often brushes his hair longer than necessary. He decides the stubble growing from his jawline can wait. He doesn't feel like shaving today, and sometimes for days and weeks. His facial hair is soft and gentle and the skin on his face is easily irritated so he delays shaving as much as he can.

Staring intently, Terve reminds himself to talk to the fields today, telling them how grateful he is and showing them with spontaneous symbols and sounds when he is around them. He is also apprising himself that he is okay, that he loves his life, and that he is grateful to find this place he calls home.

A loaf of homemade bread sits on the counter with a mason jar full of brambleberry jam, Terve's favorite. He stands in front of the toaster looking out the large windows with a front-row view of his land. Crops stand as far as the eye can see. He shifts his weight when the toaster pops and loads butter and jam onto the pieces of toast. Hot black coffee sits in a French press ready to pour into a hearty mug sitting next to it.

The kitchen, like the bathroom, feels rustic. Recycled woods along with burnt concrete and charred accents from the house that previously stood on this land were used to build his home; something he felt strongly about when he decided to build here. Although overgrown and in need of some TLC at the time, the meadow and the large forest beyond were enough for him. However, the stars of the property were three mountain ridges in the distance that were linked to a series of mountain ranges stretching for miles and miles.

In the kitchen, the large farm sink along with the open grill creates an expansive feeling. Glass, cedar, and copper-framed walls much like the bathroom bolster the sense of living outdoors. Each room is an extension of the other with similar accents. The four-by-four wooden beams overhead alternate with iron beams for support. The iron melts into the floating stairs that lead up to the master's suite. The metals and wood somehow work. The contrasting recycled woods from various trees exude forest. Expecting a tree to be growing out of the foundation would be understandable. Terve is the tree. He is grounded and centered in this space.

CHAPTER 2
ROHKEA

Breakfast complete, coffee in hand, Terve heads toward the stables. His horse, Rohkea, waits for him. Fifteen hands, Rohkea is a rich chestnut brown with flaxen mane and tail. His eyes hold the strength of his ancestors. His lineage is endless; he has been with Terve for several years. Their relationship symbiotic, strong, and magical. Terve knows Rohkea. He feels what he feels and senses what he senses and when Terve is unsure, he looks to Rohkea for assurance.

Rohkea hears Terve approaching the stable with pockets filled with carrots and apples. He exhales and smiles when Terve pokes his head inside to say hello. He opens the stable door and lets Rohkea saunter out for breakfast. This is their routine. Since Rohkea was a colt, they have carried on this way in the morning. Terve pretends he didn't bring him any treats and Rohkea steals the carrots that conspicuously hang out his back pocket. Terve acts surprised and pushes on the horse's side and they circle each other for a minute or two before walking toward his feed. Terve blows in Rohkea's left nostril a little and talks to him about life and the day he has planned.

Terve has several horses, but Rohkea is his and his alone.

"We're going to see her today," Terve says to his friend. "I know we haven't visited in a while, but farming is a full-time job, if you hadn't noticed."

Terve grabs his hat and some water for a long ride. He stuffs an oatcake in his pack along with two carrots for Rohkea. He doesn't bother locking up the house. No one else lives for miles. The hired workers that help him with the land are not working today. Planning to make this trip, he gave them the day off.

Before Terve mounts Rohkea, he lets the other horses out of their stables so they can run in the meadow. He likes to let them run off some steam and exercise without a saddle or rider. He enjoys watching the energy in their eyes shift when they know they are going to be free for the day. He feels expansive, knowing they are grateful. Although Rohkea and he will try to be back by lunch, he will let the horses roam for the day.

CHAPTER 3
BEFORE SOMEWHERE ELSE

Terve packs the final items from the house into his F-150 pickup truck. He opens the back of the extended cab and helps the twins Kali and Kaia in. They are eleven now and insist that they do not need their father's help to get in, but Terve can't resist. He feels like they are the most precious things he has in the world and can't endure any more loss. He dismisses his children's protests with extra hugs and kisses as they each enter the truck.

"Why do we have to move?" asks Kaia.

"Yeah, Dad, why do we?" Kali says.

"We've talked about this. We are starting a new adventure together, and we can't do that here," Terve tenderly says to the twins.

A final run-through of his mental checklist, and he is ready to head toward somewhere else.

He positions the rearview mirror on the two children instead of what was once their home. He doesn't want to see it disappear in the rearview. He doesn't want to let go of her. He doesn't want to do anything, but he knows that he cannot stay

here. Terve pauses and looks into the twin's eyes and sees his
dead wife's. Four teal blue seas stare back at him. The picture is
almost more than he can endure. His twins have his mouth and
smile, but their eyes and hair and cheeks are all their mother's.

CHAPTER 4
NEA'S HOME

Terve drives up the long driveway to his mother Nea's house. The children rush out of the truck the Moment it comes to a halt. Their excitement to see their grandmother means they don't wait until their dad helps them. All they see is a grandmother and she is just what these two need. Terve has his mother's eyes. Her gold rings shimmer in the sunlight. Trying to get a look at her son, she cups her hand over her forehead to make a shade. Terve knows his mother is sizing him up and avoids looking directly at her. Nea is a few inches shorter than he so her vantage point is challenged when he won't look directly at her.

"The eyes have the conversations we may not be able or ready to have," Nea often says.

Hoping to get him alone, Nea shouts "Kids, run inside. Sandwiches and cider are waiting for you on the counter."

"Awesome," Kali says.

"I'll race you there," Kaia hollers back.

Both children head for the porch, pushing and shoving to see who will get to the sandwiches first.

SONYA YOUNG

Once the twins are out of range, Nea hooks her arm into Terve's and slows his walk so he takes time to talk with her.

"Ok, Mom, let's have it," Terve says to his mother.

"Well, I was just wondering how you are doing, and if you are sure you want to do this."

"Oh, I'm sure. I couldn't stand a second more in that house without her. This is the only way I know to move forward."

"But aren't you worried the change is too fast for the children, Terve? They have barely processed their mother's passing. Then to move, all in the same year. It seems like too much for you and them."

Nea gently rubs her son's arm as she speaks, assuring him that she is not trying to attack his decision but challenge the possibility he is moving too fast. "You can't run from this, son."

"I know, Mom, but what else can I do?" Terve starts to break down.

Realizing his children are just inside, he quickly catches himself. Standing taller than before the conversation started, he turns and unloads the children's things from the truck. The kids are going to stay with his mom and dad until their new home is ready.

Nea watches her son manage his grief and wishes she could ease this part for him. She remembers him as a child, always quiet and to himself. She had to bribe him with cookies or pizza just to get him to open up to her about his feelings. Nea always knew when something was troubling him but also knew he had to develop his own way of telling her things. His wife, Teija was the catalyst for Terve's change. A gift for her son, Nea felt. Teija spoke freely and with love and kindness, knowing what to say to Terve and how to put his mind at ease. She was such a beautiful mother. The twins are drenched in her essence and, as a result, difficult at times for Terve to be around.

CHAPTER 5
SOMEWHERE ELSE

Terve rides on the wide borders that surround endless acres of farmland toward the tree line. Once a meadow, now it is an active farm filled with wheat, oats, and rice. Normally, these crops are not grown together or in the same climate, but that is the mystery of this farm.

Terve slows Rohkea as he reaches the tree lines. Before he walks into the forest, he dismounts to pick a bouquet of mountain lupine and Aspen daisies, Teija's favorite.

A family of quaking Aspen is the frontline of this forest. Most of the Aspen look young except for one which Terve signals with a quick hand gesture. Veli shakes his leaves in response. Terve met Veli years before when he first moved to the farm. Veli wanted to know who the sad man was carrying baby trees into the forest and for what purpose. Since Reya's time, no one had visited the tree line nor spoken to the Aspen. Terve's friendship, although different from Reya's, was still precious to the Aspens.

His final steps are filled with mixed emotions. When the children were younger, Terve would bring them along, but now they are grown up and living their own lives. Their visits home are staggered and often spontaneous. Terve understands it is a natural progression for his children, and instead has, over time, adopted his own rituals when he visits. Before rounding the corner, he pauses before entering and remembers the first time he visited this place.

He was grieving. The children were still with his parents as he prepared this new place to live. He was grieving for their company as well as the loss of his wife and their life together, grieving for the life they would never have, and for the irreparable harm losing their mother would do his twins. He takes a deep breath and releases Rohkea to meander just a few more steps and, with his exhale, the forest opens into a sanctuary.

As a first act in his new home, Terve created this memorial site for his wife who passed away many years ago.

Three Japanese maple trees and three pink weeping cherry trees create a circle. Large rocks rest in front of the trees, and in the center of the circle, a headstone that reads:

A Gift, A Bright Light, A Friend & Mother
Forever Missed
Teija Summer

CHAPTER 6
GLIMPSE INTO THE UNKNOWN

Multiple-sized rings suspended vertically in space.
Hinged in the same spot by an invisible link.
Revolving counterclockwise on an invisible track.
Each ring slightly smaller than the previous ring so they fit inside each other.
Individually the circles rotate 360 degrees.
Each ring releases with it a silky sheer curtain-like veil.
The veil travels in the same motion as the circle, rising and falling,
Caressing the space at the 180-degree mark then lifting back up.
The rings, working from the largest to the innermost, repeat this motion endlessly.

CHAPTER 7
TERVE'S CIRCLE

LASNA AND VIIME SWITCH PLACES WHILE TULEVAISUUS SLEEPS.
TULEVAISUUS IS GOING TO BE SURPRISED WHEN HE WAKES, VIIME
SAYS. LASNA CHUCKLES AND ROCKS SLIDE DOWN HER SIDES.

Rohkea hovers a bit while Terve sits with his head lowered in
quiet contemplation. He stopped praying years ago when he
lost his wife. Instead, he practices quiet moments of appreciation and gratitude. He regularly takes time to sit and mindfully
account for the things at present he is grateful for. Initially, in
the heat of grief and despair, he often could only muster one or
two things a day. Often those two things turned out to be his
children. Over time, however, these moments evolved into long
talks with himself, his feelings, and how he sensed himself in
the home he made. Creating this place to honor his wife turned
out to be his space, too. His respite when overwhelmed, Terve

would ride Rohkea out here and converse with nature as nature spoke back.

Always connected to nature, especially trees, he decided to create this memorial place here instead of closer to his home in the meadow.

Today, feeling nostalgic, he remembers when he was a little boy at home with his mom and dad. He would sit in a big oak tree and stare over the horizon for hours and hours. Often a way to escape the eyeshot of his mother, Terve felt like he was a hawk watching the world from above. Time evaporated back then. He was sitting in that oak tree when the first symbols arrived on his arms. He recalled sitting on a tree limb where he nestled himself close to the body of the tree so he wouldn't fall off. He did this often so he could stay up there longer. That day, however, he fell asleep and dreamt that the tree he was sitting on came alive and picked him up off the ground, pulled him in close, and held him like he was a baby being held by his mother. The swaying motion in the dream pushed him deeper into delta waves. For eternity he felt unconditional love from Aiti, the tree. The kind of love that fills up all the space in your body expanding to the point you feel you might pop. Terve loved the way the tree made him feel safe. As the tree held him, she told him stories and whispered things in his ear only he could hear. As the tree spoke to him, lighted symbols surrounded his body, moving around his hands, feet, and head.

Flashes of a meadow, a forest, and three mountain ridges played in front of Terve's eyes, like a movie. He saw a woman with a large dog running in a field jumping and playing. She had brownish black hair and what looked like a bad haircut. As the picture zoomed in closer, the woman's right hand was filled with seeds and blossoms. She was holding them tenderly and tapping her thumb to her fourth finger while putting her left hand on her heart. She was rocking slowly, just like the tree holding him was. Terve could feel what she felt and hear what she heard. The plants were speaking to her somehow, and she was getting to know them like a friend or a relative.

When the symbols and lights around Terve finished dancing, they began branding his skin with light. He felt each one enter him, some painful, some exciting, some tragic, but some so joy-filled he could barely stand it. Releasing him from her embrace, Aiti stroked his back, coaxing him to wake up. Just barely awake, now small, sweet, innocent Terve realizes he had fallen asleep. In the moment just before he becomes conscious, he hears a voice say,

"Reya, you dear, sweet girl!"

Snapping upright, Terve looks side to side for who just spoke. Seeing no one, he realizes that he must have still been dreaming. He wants to jump out of the tree and tell his mom, but his arm fell asleep during his dream and he must shake it awake. Looking down at his hand, he sees the symbols on his arm. He's seen these symbols before on his mom and dad.

Excited to show his parents, Terve jumps out of the tree and runs to the house, shouting, "Mom, Dad, look at my arms!"

CHAPTER 8
SOMEWHERE ELSE – A FRESH START

The twins, distracted by Nea, barely lifted their heads to tell Terve goodbye as he headed out to create their new home. The property was only about thirty miles from his parents' home so he knew he could drive there to see them often. Reportedly, no one had lived on the land for over forty years. A terrible fire destroyed the buildings along with the surrounding fields and forest. Abe, Terve's real estate agent, didn't give him much information about what happened. The property, now owned by the bank, was a purchase "as is" deal, an issue discouraging previously interested buyers. Abe tells Terve that the property was purchased after the fire by a man who refused to sell it because of its sentimental value. When he passed away with no heirs, the bank reclaimed the property. Abe said he never understood why someone hadn't taken a chance on the place. The acreage was endless and the view:

"Well, who wouldn't want this view of the mountains?" Abe wondered, studying Terve's reaction.

As soon as he arrives, Terve slides out of the F-150 and

heads toward the clearing crew he has scheduled to meet him. Philip, the crew's foreman, walks toward him.

"Are you ready to get started?" Philip asks.

"Ready as I will ever be. My plan is to repurpose and recycle anything useable from the previous home."

Philip looked at Terve like he was crazy. He didn't believe there would be much salvageable but felt it best that Terve discover that on his own. Excited about what he might find on the grounds, Terve anxiously follows the team's progress. He felt strongly that he wouldn't know how to position his new home until he could see the cleared and cleaned site. In the meantime, he decided to find a place to pitch his tent. His plan was to spend day and night on the property to expedite finishing it so he could bring his children home.

Bulldozers, backhoes, and a team of landscape experts attacked the property. Peeling back layer after layer of time, they revealed sweetness Terve could feel radiating from where the house once stood. The feeling reminded him of something he just couldn't place but he recognized. Although his memories failed him, his tattoos burned a little to remind him.

VIIME, LASNA, AND TULEVAISUUS ALL WAKE UP TOGETHER. THEY FEEL SOMETHING IN THE AIR AND WANT TO FIND OUT WHAT CAUSED A STIR IN THE EARTH TODAY.

Terve hammers in the final peg of his tent and decides to take a walk. The equipment is loud and intense. He thought about asking Philip for the protective gear for his ears but decides a walk is a better choice. Pushing through the overgrown cheatgrass and Canadian thistle, Terve attempts to put some distance between himself and the noise. He's glad he wore his heavy-duty hiking boots today because the property is infested with the invasive grass. He wonders briefly if the grass had anything to do with the fire, but quickly brushes it off and heads for the wide-open meadow.

As he makes his way farther from the property and the noise, he struggles to find a walking trail or a path to navigate the dense meadow. Slowly and methodically, he talks to the property. His affinity for nature increased after the branding occurred. He reaches out and his hand hovers over the tops of the tall grass and wildflowers. Terve feels a wheel start moving inside of him. The motion makes a low hum. He feels the grass feeling him and he knows that the land is talking to him. Reaching deep within the soil across many lives, the meadow holds the stories of many, but very few have heard them. He closes his eyes and tunes in to the space. He gently lowers his eyelids and sees a roaring cloud of bees coming toward him. They are traveling together, flying in formation; each movement felt by the others. The slightest twitch and the bees shift, breaking formation and spreading out all over the meadow, but this is the older meadow, not the one Terve was just standing in. Instead of old wreckage needing a clearing crew, he sees a small greenhouse with beehives on the edge of the meadow. The garden is humble and looks like just enough to feed a family. He could smell honey. As he remains still, the hum turns into a whisper, a voice saying, "Reya, come home."

Startled, he pulls his hand back. Recognition returns. He remembers the dream in the tree and the woman with the dog in the meadow. Terve pulls his ballcap off his head slowly and looks up, seeing the mountains in the background as if for the first time. He trembles inside and releases some of the grief that has rooted inside him. He thought it was a dream that day in the tree. He never believed that forty years later he would see the mountains in person.

FEELING HIS EMOTIONS, LASNA PUSHES VIIME TO SKIP ROCKS OVER TULEVAISUUS' HEAD. THE MOUNTAINS CHUCKLE, AND THE EARTH QUIVERS A LITTLE.

CHAPTER 9

SOMEWHERE ELSE – A HOME TO BUILD

The crew left for the day, hauling off most of the dead plants, overgrown grass, and weeds. Philip honored Terve's request and stacked remains from the home: several hunks of wood, beams, and items. There was still a lot of work to do.

"Day One," Terve says to himself as he looks at a spot that is supposed to become the new home for his family.

Normally when looking at what might become a lengthy problem, Terve might feel doubt and fear. He does now, but he also feels the excitement in the pit of his stomach. The incident in the field he had earlier that afternoon soothed the doubt a little. He still didn't know how he knew that it was the right thing for him to be here in this moment. Terve grabs his cooler out of the truck and sits on the tailgate. He pulls out a turkey sandwich Nea made him with some vinegar and salt kettle chips along with a cold IPA. Nea knew he loved her brownies, so she packed four large chunky ones, too. Eating his sandwich, he looked out at the mountains and big sky and challenged himself to imagine the possibilities. Imagine a new life here and what that might look like. What smells will he hold for the rest of his life that are born here? What sounds and songs will the twins make playing in the yard out back? What will love bring to this space? His heart swells a little as if it's too much to process today.

"Day One," he whispers to himself again.

The last drop of beer slides down his throat. He pulls the bottle back as if looking at it did not convince him it was empty. He peers into the cooler but only water remains. Glancing at the tent, he decides that the day has caught up to him and it's time to turn in. He looks at his cell phone. Nea sent him text messages with pictures of the kids playing outside. She knew they would be in his thoughts today.

"Thanks, Mom," he texts back.

Dreaming:

Terve is in a car which is hovering for a Moment then moving vertically. He looks up to see where. He watches his body and vehicle move up into a floating city. The buildings are hovering in the air. How is this possible? Where is this possible? Terve's still moving effortlessly through the city when he sees a circle of trees below. Some sort of shrine or an open park. People are sitting outside on benches made of marble or some sort of stone. The city is so clean. It feels light and airy here. The car moves closer to the trees. There are seven trees: three red, three pink, and one odd-looking tree in the center. A woman is standing in front of the odd-looking tree, making hand gestures to it. She is tall and very thin, frail almost. Long silver-grey braids flow down her back. She is wearing a long, soft buttery-yellow colored cottony skirt with a plush wrap around her shoulders. Her left palm faces up, flat, with the fourth finger on her right hand drawing a circle counterclockwise on her palm. He is talking to himself inside the dream.

"Come on. Come on. Come on, turn around so I can see your face."

The woman, as if hearing him, starts to turn. Terve strains his eyes to see as she slowly begins making another gesture. As her profile comes into view the picture begins to fade to nothingness.

LASNA PINCHES TULEVAISUUS WHILE HE SLEEPS.

Loud trucks pulling up the dirt driveway wake him. For a moment, Terve forgot he was in a tent without any running water or coffee.

"Oh, shit, I forgot the coffee," he said out loud.

Kicking himself, Terve decides that he is going to have to work out some things if he is going to stay here and supervise the work.

Philip sees Terve moving about, talking to himself. He offers him a cup of coffee and a breakfast burrito. Terve almost trips in his eagerness for the food and coffee.

"Thanks, Philip!" Terve says as he shoves burrito in his mouth.

"I want to walk the foundation with you today, if that is okay," Philip tells him. "I need you to tell me exactly what we are supposed to repurpose and also get a rough idea of which direction you want to face the property, etc."

Terve nods and sips coffee while they head toward the foundation, engaging in small talk. Philip, not convinced, asks Terve if he really slept in that tent all night. Terve snickers a little and tells him about having weird dreams.

Philip excuses himself to talk to the crew, and Terve starts to walk the property. Beneath the overgrown grass and weeds, charred remnants of what once stood here are visible. Parts of the concrete foundation revealed the direction of the fire and its intensity. The dark echoes embedded in the foundation seemed beautiful to him. He wants to keep the original concrete for the aesthetics if possible. However, the concrete had so many cracks and vulnerabilities in it they might need to replace the existing with new.

Moving along the outline of the foundation he saw fresh cracks. You could tell they were new because they were not yet filled with dirt or debris. As Terve got closer, he glimpsed some metal. He slipped his fingers through the crack and felt something. He looked around, but Philip was still giving the crew directions, so Terve decided to dig further. The cracks helped because he was able to slide several pieces of concrete away to enlarge the opening.

Pulling away one more piece, Terve cut his finger on the jagged edges of the concrete. A drop of blood seeps out of his finger. As he draws his finger closer to his mouth, he smells vanilla and butterscotch. He closes his eyes and places his finger against his tongue to lick off the blood. A flash of light and Terve sees a row of plants shining in bright light. He feels himself make the motion with his lips before he speaks it out loud.

"Reya?"

The blood stopped quickly and Terve clears the last piece of concrete, allowing him to free a metal box. There isn't a lock on it. Fireproof, of course, Terve thought as he picks it up. He feels movement inside the box. How could this be left behind? He pushes off the dust and dirt and years-old caked-on burnt residue. Something inside him feels it best to wait to open it when he is alone. He walks the metal box back to his truck and slips it in the back seat.

Philip finished passing on instructions and rejoins Terve as he continues walking the property.

CHAPTER 10
GLIMPSE INTO THE UNKNOWN

Space endless space.
Ribbons of Prussian and cerulean blue along with white gold form
massive waterspouts
The size of the moon rotating clockwise.
A low hum emanates from the spout as it moves forward toward an
unknown destination.
White seeds, saplings, and blossoms manifest in between the ribbons of
color.
The force of the rotation launches blossoms along with the saplings and
seeds into infinity.
Each one disappears with a tiny little explosion of light.

CHAPTER 11
THE BOX

Terve said goodbye to Philip for the day. He was off to schedule the inspection for the foundation and the rest of the property to find out what was going to have to be replaced entirely and what might be salvaged. Philip wasn't optimistic that anything would be worth saving after seeing the condition of the old home site. His initial observations were that a new foundation had to be poured for sure. He wouldn't share his feeling with Terve until he had confirmation, but Philip had many years of experience and felt confident that Terve would be starting over completely. The only things Philip thought salvageable were the property and the stunning view.

Terve waved as the last truck pulled away from the would-be driveway and headed for his tent. He decided today that he would spend one more night on the property and then head back to his mother's until Philip got some of the plumbing in place. Terve loved the outdoors and didn't mind camping, but he also loved his morning shower and could barely tolerate missing it. This decision would make his days longer for a while but getting to see his kids more often would be a welcome gift.

Earlier, while the crew took lunch, Terve grabbed the metal

box out of his back seat and set it on the tailgate, planning to look inside. He held it for a little while, studying it and attempting to figure out how to get it open. It had a rusted and decayed spring on it. A couple of dents on the top made it difficult to pry open with his hands. He rummaged through his cab to find a flat-head screwdriver. With a little will power and strength, Terve pried the dents open, loosening the lid. With great anticipation, he lifted the rusted latch slowly and it crumbled apart with the motion. He wondered that the latch lasted so long. When he got the lid off, he was overcome with smells. Flowers and fruits and honey. Blackberries and thyme were the first that his senses recognized. Following that were carrots, wax beans, lavender and lemons, oats and bran, maple, and bananas. One after another, the smells continued to flow out of the box. Distracted by the smells, he hadn't noticed the little envelopes nor the leather notebook. The notebook was partially rolled up like it was forced in the box as a hurried afterthought, and the pages were a little wrinkled as a result. He knew before he touched it who it belonged to.

"Reya," Terve said, whispering under his voice as if fearing she would materialize if he said it out loud. He carefully flattened the notebook, realizing touching it may make it disintegrate. Water damage around the edges of the leather gave Terve concern for the contents. He delicately peeled the leather away from the first pages and read:

Reya's Exploration into Nature

Terve took pause, grasping the impact this Moment might have on his life. He knew instinctively that if he opened the notebook even one more page, his life would never be the same. He knew that once he turned that first page, he would be unable to deny what he knew was a profound experience. Delighted and fearful, he sat with the notebook for a while, staring at it. He placed it beside himself and looked out over his property. The mountains looked different than moments earlier when he first sat down, as if their shapes or ridges changed. He thought the angle of the sun must have shifted. Terve returned to considering his life and the life he wanted to build here on this property.

VIIME, LASNA AND TULEVAISUUS STOPPED PLAYING AND LOOKED DOWN OVER THE PROPERTY. THEY FELT A STIRRING IN THE SPACE THAT THEY HADN'T FELT SINCE REYA LIVED ON THE LAND. CURIOUS, THEY CLIMBED OVER EACH OTHER TO SCOPE OUT THE BEST VIEW OF THE HAPPENINGS BELOW.

Terve sat, watching and listening to the silence fall over his property. The absence of sound was deafening and calming. He could finally hear himself breathe unrestricted. It felt good and sad because he thought that his wife would have loved this place, too. They had lived closer to town for her job as a lawyer and the children's school, but both imagined that one day they would spend more time closer to his parents and the outdoors. Terve told her he wanted to have a little farm and grow some food and tinker around in the yard. He wanted to teach the children about nature as he had learned as a boy. He told his wife that the tattoos on his body were a result of playing with nature and that he felt he might pass the same things to the twins. She didn't understand why she or anyone else who played in nature didn't have them too. Terve couldn't explain to her why but he knew that the symbols couldn't be given away nor passed to anyone. The symbols and signs come to whom they choose.

Terve said a silent prayer to himself and his wife. I asked for a change, he thought, and now is the time to stand in that. Own that. Believe in it and know that everything I ever wanted is right here.

When his heart decided to open the next page in the notebook, the tattoos on his arms began to vibrate.

"Here we go," he said.

"Day 2," Terve read.

CHAPTER 12
REYA'S NOTEBOOK

The initial page had a few notes in it.

This place is magical. The meadow and the trees are alive, and I am in love with finding out all the little unknowns. I have so many questions, I might explode. Questions like:

Where do the lights come from?

Are seeds alive?

Does the grass want to be my friend?

Can I play with the bees without getting stung?

Does my heart hear voices or am I crazy?

I am never leaving this place. Valo and I can hardly believe we are so lucky to live here. I am home.

He closes the book and picks up one of the envelopes. He hears movement inside it. Using the screwdriver, Terve opens the envelope on the seam. He doesn't wish to harm anything of value inside. Once he's confident, he opens the envelope and looks inside. The same aromas from when he opened the metal box came to tickle his nose. A little difficult to see the inside, he decides to slowly tilt it upward to force out the contents.

Little envelopes, sachets, and clippings fall out onto the truck bed. You can feel the love and tenderness taken to package the items. She must have felt they were important, Terve imagines. As he picks up one of the envelopes, he sees a flash that his eyes follow to the wild meadow as it is replaced with rows of crops. A huge farm lay before him: thriving, busy, and alive. A quickly as it appears, it vanishes into his consciousness. He didn't know how or why or when but he knows that he is going to farm the land here. Arms tingling and the hairs on his neck at attention, Terve looks at the mountains again. They have changed once more. Scratching his head, he says, "It's been a long day."

Terve packs up the truck and decides to drive to his parents to sleep instead of camping and, more importantly, take a shower.

CHAPTER 13

A NEW HOME

While the construction was coming to an end on his dream home, Terve spent many hours deciphering Reya's notebook. The book was filled with drawings of symbols, some matching the symbols on his arms while others were new to him. She also had intimate descriptions of her identification of certain plants. The descriptions were loving and kind. He could feel her sense of discovery while reading each page. Sometimes he would find just a few lines for recipes or combinations to make soaps and scrubs. Terve could tell the notebook was a dear possession. So dear, that he wasn't sure why it was left behind. He could feel Reya in the pages.

He imagined her there in the same space looking at the same view of the mountains and wondered if she felt the way he did. Sometimes when he would turn a page, symbols on his arms and fingers would buzz. Like little bees singing, somehow the pages were for him or connected to him. He wondered if Reya also had markings and experiences she couldn't explain. So, he read on and looked deeper for answers about the mystery woman. Unfortunately, Reya's writings came to an unexpected end. Her notes were not finished. You could feel it in the way the writing just stopped. It was as if she placed the notebook on the table and forgot to return to it. Terve felt a slight pull in his chest. He felt a little robbed of answers he assumed he would find in the pages.

Philip got the electricity and water going so Terve spent a lot more time on the site instead of driving back and forth. He wanted to expedite the completion date so that he and the kids could begin their new adventure.

He showered outside in a makeshift shower which he had put together on the fly. He enjoyed the feeling so much being outdoors that he had Philip change the original plans for his master bathroom so that the shower felt open and accessible to nature. He wanted the shower to feel like showering outside as he is now, waiting for the home to be finished.

Terve walked the overgrown meadow most days and talked to himself and the land about the farm he would manifest. On one of his walks on the border of the property, he came across the remains of what looked like beehives. Bees were long gone from the hives, just pieces and parts really, but he could tell it had been a small grouping of hives. Terve hovered his hand over the space where they once stood. Since childhood, he would hover his hands over a space if he wanted to know more about it. He told his mother, Nea, that he was tuning into it. The buzzing feeling grew and grew until he thought it might be possible the bees were still present.

"You will be again," he said to the hives, and immediately added that to his dreams for the farm. He would become just like Reya and bees would thrive here again.

As he pushed forward into the field, he could see an opening to the forest just beyond a row of Aspen trees.

"It can't be. Could it?"

Terve slows his walk. Reya's notebook mentions a family of Aspen trees, but they would have surely perished in the massive fire. He approaches the oldest looking tree and extends his right hand as if saying hello but instead his fingers begin opening as far as they will stretch and then closing.

While doing this motion, Terve looks at the grown tree and whispers, "You must be Veli."

The trees do not respond right away. He moves closer to the father tree and touches him with both hands. He leans forward and wraps his arms around the trunk of the tree, steps back, and opens his hand with his palm supine and opening toward the tree. He stays in this position until his body moves him to bow before the tree.

Words come up through his body that are not his, but sound like him.

"Veli, I am Terve and I am going to bring this place back to life. I am going to fill the fields with love and kindness and allow the essence of Reya to flow through this space again."

Terve hears a whisper on the wind or coming from the space around him.

"You will do more than that, Terve. You will bring about a change in the world that you never expected possible."

Still unsure where the voice is coming from, he slowly turns in a circle and shrugs his shoulders, responding, "Do you mean by farming?"

He felt ridiculous. As a child, Terve talked to the wind and the water and plants but had stopped once he reached adolescence. He felt uncomfortable sharing that side of himself with other kids. The markings on his body were enough to try to explain away without telling them he could feel the animals and plants.

The whisper returned, "You, like Reya, are special. You can access the connection of our space with yours."

"Who was she? What happened here?" Terve demanded from the whisper.

"There will be time for that, Terve. For now, it is just good to see you are here. Even the mountains are curious, and those guys hardly move for anyone. Consider it an honor that you are being noticed."

Terve scratches his head and ponders how Reya's trees could survive the massive fire. There were still charred marks evident on trees that lay beyond the row of Aspen. Some trees lay on the ground, unable to stand any longer. Some sprouted new growth from partially burned trunks and branches. The forest had recovered from the fire, but hints of it remained. Terve made a note of the downed trees, deciding to have Philip bring guys out here to gather any of them that could be useful. He wanted to put some to use in the house and the stables.

The whisper continues, "We survived because our root system remains connected to the Unknown. It is that strong connection that allows us to return life after life. We don't look exactly like we did in Reya's time, but our connection and roots to this place are the same. "

"That's amazing," Terve smiles and looks toward the rest of the forest. He holds the notebook tighter and thanks Reya for leaving it behind. He begins talking out loud to Veli, assuming he can hear and understand.

"She left this notebook in a box along with packets of seeds."

Veli and his children shake their leaves and lean in toward him, the first indication that they can hear or notice him.

"I am not sure what I should do with them," Terve continued, "She said that she could never get them to grow, but she also said they were important because Aiti told her."

Frustrated, Terve looks up and says, "I don't even know who Aiti is. She must have been very important to Reya because she says that she felt guilty for letting Aiti down."

The whisper responds, "Sometimes things are misinterpreted or misunderstood. In such times, we are left feeling doubtful or inadequate. But Reya was never that. At least not to any of us here in the forest. She gave all that she had available at that time to this land."

Lasna climbs over Viime to get a closer look at the man walking in the fields.

As he walks back toward his homesite, he hears a heartbeat in his head. The heartbeat does not feel like his own. It feels like the heartbeat is outside himself, but he can hear it inside. Terve stops, eyes skimming the tops of the overgrown grass in the meadow. He hears crying and doesn't know where it is coming from.

There. He sees her on her hands and knees digging little holes in the ground one after another. She is lowering dirt into the soil. It doesn't make sense to him, but he continues to watch. All the while the heartbeat is going inside his head. She places small purple blossoms on top of each little mound of soil. He wonders if this is some weird practice. Who buries dirt in the dirt, he wonders? He strains to listen to her whisper. She is apologizing for something. Her head raises and she looks across the meadow. He waves to her, but she cannot see him. Instantly, he is surrounded by mounds of little graves of dirt with purple flowers on them. They are endless, but he can't imagine what they are for. She looks defeated, sobbing on the dirt. He feels drawn to her somehow and tries to run to her and hold her, but he cannot move. Her tears fall into the soil, and, as if switching on a light, the tears turn on an underground network of light.

The seeds are beneath the soil. They are alive. The heartbeat he hears is theirs. They are waiting and watching.

Butterflies and hummingbirds surround her along with a large dog. She pets him gently and returns to her backyard. Terve follows her with his eyes. The yard is filled with a beautiful garden. Fresh flowers fill the perimeter, the smell of thyme and basil in the air. He likes this place she made. As if hearing something, she looks over her shoulder and pauses at her door. He can see her. It is Reya standing there, clear as day. He can see her beautiful home and feel her love. It is a love so powerful that it takes his breath away, and he feels himself falling forward. He cannot stop the motion. He thinks he will face plant for sure, but when his body just meets the earth, the picture fades and he is back in the meadow. Alone.

Terve takes a moment to process, and instantly misses his wife. The experience leaves him electrified. The network below his feet is alive and waiting. Intuitively, he knows that it is waiting for the right person to hit the switch. Calmness washes over him and Terve notices that sprinkled throughout the field are purple and yellow Aspen daisies and violet mountain lupine. As he discerns the motion, his arms light up, and his hands rise, palms together as if praying, leaving a small space between them. He bows his head and acknowledges the meadow and the network.

Philip approaches Terve calmly. He can tell he is deep in thought and doesn't want to disturb him in prayer.

"We are about done here. I just need to go over some final things with you. Do you have time now?"

"Sure," Terve says as he scratches his head a bit and shakes off the Moments before.

Philip tells him that they just have some landscaping and painting to do along with lighting and they should be good to move in by the end of the week.

"My guys would like to get started on the stables for your

horses. Also, I'll need some input about what type of irrigation system you want."

"I'll grab my cooler out of the truck and meet you on the porch."

"Great." Philip adds. "I need to be ready; they are bringing in the appliances and installing the huge farm sink you wanted."

Philip and he spent an hour hashing out items about the stables. When they finish, Terve heads out to pick up a quick bite for supper. He selects an outdoor café at a farm not far from him. He brought along the notes from Reya.

I can feel the space around the flowers. When I put my hands near the flowers, I can feel them draw me into them. I felt like I was going to fall into the face of the echinacea. I leaned in close. I wanted to see if I could hear it. I felt my feet falling forward like I was slipping into something that was there, but I couldn't see it.

Terve flips through the pages lightly. He is remembering when he was a child and did the same thing. "Why did I ever stop playing with nature?"

The seeds won't grow. I try and try to get them to germinate but each time I plant them, nothing happens. Kuriiri continues to give me more packets of seeds, but still no luck. Aiti will be so disappointed in me. I continue to bury them in the meadow, but I can't help feeling like a failure. There must be something I am not seeing or feeling. The rest of my garden prospers.

Terve says, "Oh, that must be what she was doing. She was burying the seeds. Wait, but they are still alive," he says to himself.

"That's terrible," he considers. She thinks she killed them. That's why she was crying in the field. Wow. Terve inches back in his chair and contemplates the reality. How hard that must have been; to try and try and try and never feel like you have succeeded even when you put your whole heart and soul into it.

Each page becomes more precious to him. He hesitates to think about the next page.

Pistachio and Pomegranate Salad
Steam kale on the stovetop. Drain and place in a cold bath. Chop finely. Toss with pomegranate arils and chopped pistachio and a drizzle of basil-infused olive oil. Top with fresh parmesan cheese. Serve with whole wheat and oat toast with lime and honey butter.

This sounds great, he thinks. He looks at the café menu and finds a beet salad that sounds good. He orders a chicken pesto sandwich with a beet salad and sweet potato fries on the side.

He bites into the pesto sandwich and the taste explodes in his mouth. As if waking up again for the first time, Terve is drawn into the sandwich.

"I must be starving."

He laughs inside a little. It is not his stomach, but his senses. It is like waking up from a long sleep. Losing his wife, and his life, left him hopeless until he found this property and began to discover the land and its stories. For the first time in a long time, Terve feels good. He still longs for Teija. He doesn't think he will ever get over that feeling, but at least he has focus right now, and for that he is grateful.

I get a funny feeling in the meadow. I feel like I am being watched by someone or something. I brush it off most days, but there are times I feel that if I could just break through the boundary that separates me from whatever it is, we could meet for real. Sometimes I think it is she, the lady in the dream of the floating city.

"Sir, can I get you anything else today? Sir?" the waitress waits for Terve to snap out of it. His mind is somewhere else, and she patiently waits for him to return.

"Huh? Wait! What?" Terve stumbles with his words.

"I just wanted to know if you are ready for your check," she says.

"Yes, I am. Thanks. I'll take the check."

CHAPTER 14
FINISHING TOUCHES

The house looks remarkable. It is just what he had hoped for: with the inside and the outside in complete synchrony, a ranch style with additions on both ends of the house; one end for the twins and game rooms, and the other the master suite and office. Terve is impressed with how Philip's crew repurposed so many things from the original structure along with some of the wood from the forest. In Philip's supporting Terve's desire to repurpose materials, he created a masterpiece. The slanted dark slate-grey roof was repurposed metal with solar panels attached. The center of the house was cedar with large picture windows to continue the flow inside out. Each separate end unit was fashioned from repurposed cargo cars stacked geometrically on top of each other to create separate floors. The freight cars were painted a medium grey-blue tone that popped against the large cedar beams and accents. Gas lamps lit the entryway with cedar columns supporting the porch that extended out toward the farm. Rocking chairs strategically positioned on the porch invite any onlookers to have a seat and take it all in.

Terve wanted the farm to be the focal point so he insisted on minimalistic landscaping. A mix of river rocks gives the illusion of flowing water moving toward the fields. Patches of citronella grass and wildflowers define borders for the flowing rocks but also were a reminder of the meadow that once inhabited the same spot the fields do now.

"Philip outdid himself on this project," Terve said out loud.

Terve's mother is bringing Kali and Kaia in two days to move them in. He is having a housewarming party for them. They are going to love their bedrooms. He used repurposed woods for their beds and shiplap for the walls and some of the built-in cabinets.

Looking at his watch, he realizes time is slipping away from him. The landscapers are following him into the forest this morning. He has a surprise for the kids and wants it to be ready when they arrive. He walks downstairs to look out for the landscapers and decides he has some time to walk the property.

Transformed, the once overgrown wildfire-touched foundation is an amazing residence. All the overgrown grass and weeds were removed and composted.

The beehives line the east side of the property where he erected a wall with plenty of shade to keep them cool. The wall consists of a partial trellis that allows climbing roses to grow up and around it. On opposite ends of the trellis is Italian cypress for extra cover from the wind. The bees won't be delivered until after the kids arrive and he has time to teach them the dos and don'ts associated with the hives. He hopes that they will enjoy having them and want to learn more about taking care of them.

Following in Reya's footsteps, he contacted a local honey beekeeper and offered him access to his farm in exchange for a share in the honey. To encourage other bees, Terve collected trees knocked down in storms or by lightning and took them to a local craftsman to make one hundred bee hotels. He hung the hotels around the forest and his property. Additionally, he delivered the remaining hotels to locals he had met since he began building his home. He asked them to find space for the hotel around their own home, attaching to each hotel a little bit of Reya's story about the single solitary bee that visited her.

He wanted the farm to be a pivotal place in the community and felt protecting bees was an opportunity to introduce his family along with the farm to the community.

Surveying the acres, he walks to the center of the property and stands still. Recognizing all of the hard work thus far, he is challenging himself to give his children a life neither they nor he could believe was possible. He looks at freshly tilled soil and contemplates the various crops he wants to plant. The landscapers are delivering some seeds and saplings to get him started. He isn't quite sure how he will create the vision he saw of the farm. At this point, he is trying to figure out where to plant the seeds left behind by Reya. He has plans for a handful, but since he doesn't know what is in each packet, he is unsure where to plant them.

TULEVAISUUS JUMPS ON LASNA AND PULLS ON HIS SHOULDERS.

Suspended in thought, he hears a voice on the inside whisper, "You are a man of men, and you will succeed here."

He plants his feet firmly on the ground and with a flash, an opening appears in front of his eyes. It appears as if someone took an unknown place and overlaid it on his property. He rubs his eyes a little, slightly distracted by a hum. Terve feels like he can reach out and touch the opening but when he does, he feels nothing except air. He sees a greenhouse, a large greenhouse, filled with everything. Terve feels the Greenhouse. It's an odd thing to admit to himself: he is feeling a place he doesn't know. The Greenhouse looks unusual, though. The walls do not look exactly like the ones he is used to. The walls shimmer in the light, giving the space a feeling of transparency. It's like the walls are there but also, they are not. Regardless, the Greenhouse feels familiar, so he holds his breath hoping to keep the image and the feeling as long as possible. He gasps for air finally and the space begins to dissipate. With just the space of a window remaining, firefly like lights linger in the air before it finally closes. Squinting, he thinks he must be dehydrated. He feels hot all over, and the palms of his hands are on fire. He rubs his hands on his jeans and tries to shake off the unstable feeling. Each day he is here, Terve discovers more about the land and himself.

With a strength of purpose he's never felt before, he walks toward the landscapers as they arrive. He feels invigorated and excited about the possibilities to come.

Ryan jumps out of the lead truck to shake hands with Terve.

"Why don't you ride with me so you can direct us to the location," Ryan tells him.

Ryan's team carried with them six young trees: three Japanese maples and three pink weeping cherry trees. The trees were Teija's favorites. Walking in the forest a few weeks ago, he stumbled upon an area that had huge rocks in a circle. It looked like a campsite or conceivably a sacred place for prayer, but the damage from the fire was such that he was unsure about previous use.

Terve had an idea that this might be a wonderful spot to place Teija's cremains. He envisioned a meditative garden with her favorite trees encircling her. The children and he could take hikes out and visit her. He imagined them picnicking there or camping overnight. He wanted the children to remember her. This may be the way he could continue to keep her spirit alive in their life.

He led the crew to the spot and reminded Ryan what he wanted on the site. They would plant the six trees just outside the circle of rocks, matching each tree with a rock. Fresh mulch would surround the trees and extend four feet behind them. He wanted a distinct border recognizable to those who entered. A second circle would lie inside the border of the rocks where Teija's cremains would be scattered. He purchased wildflower packets for the children to scatter inside this circle. In the very center, a placard would sit on the ground:

A Gift, A Bright Light, A Friend & Mother
Forever Missed
Teija Summer

Terve enriched the soil in the center with fertilizers from the landscapers' trucks. He would have the children come with him and his parents to sprinkle Teija's ashes on the land. For now, he took this time for himself. The landscapers busy digging holes for the trees didn't pay any attention to Terve.

He removed from his jean's pocket one of the envelopes left behind by Reya. He took a few of the seeds out of the packet and placed them gently into the soil in the center of the garden. Terve hopes for a beautiful flower to grow from the seeds. He imagines something sweet like his wife. He wanted to surprise her while giving life to these little guys. If Reya is out there watching, maybe it would bring her some sense of peace that her hard work wasn't for naught.

Terve raised his hand over the covered seeds, palm down, and began rotating it over the soil. He felt his tattoos respond. He said a little prayer silently.

"May your life be filled with the joy found in this earth. May your journey be bountiful. May you prosper."

After the landscapers left, Terve undressed and walked into his new shower. He loves the changes that Phillip made. It feels like showering outside, and the juniper haystack butterflies encircling the ceiling reinforce that delightful feeling.

CHAPTER 15
ANNIVERSARY

A year later, the farm is booming, with the help of the
community. Terve set up the farm nicely this first year. A
modest farm store, an improvised portion of a cargo unit they
didn't use on the house, sits near the roadside. Kali and Kaia,
under Nea's delighted supervision, help him run the store
during peak hours. They both have become quite the farmers
and have also blossomed into happy children again. They do
miss their mother, but all things considered, Terve is grateful
for their resilience.

For his first year, he selected sturdy crops. Crops that didn't
require as much knowledge and ones that were known to thrive
in their area. Out in the main fields, he grew beets, swiss chard,
kale, onions, potatoes, garlic, and carrots. He grew strawberries
in spring, and watermelons, cucumbers, and various types of
heirloom tomatoes in summer. Plenty of seasonal crops were
sold at the farm store. Local restaurants started requesting
specific heirloom crops. Sometimes they would bring him the
seeds and ask him to set aside land just for them. A problem he
couldn't imagine a year ago: he needed to expand.

Sarah, the local beekeeper he contracted with, said her bees were thriving on his land. Their hives were producing double what they normally produce. She attributed the abundance to the love that Terve had for the bees along with the added food sources his farm offered them. Since Terve passed out the bee hotels, Sarah's business took off, too. More people like Terve in the community reached out to her to invest in hives. This little microcosm of a community had a buzz about it that no one could pinpoint but unconsciously they could feel the environment around them shifting. Terve, minus a few jars kept for his family, sold the honey in the farm store. He labeled their honey *Reya's Harvest*. Whenever anyone inquired, he shared with them about a woman who lived on the land many moons ago and fell in love with one bee so wanted to change the world for them. Portions of the proceeds he funneled back into building more bee hotels and education programs to support Sarah's business.

Terve, unaware of it, was building a network in his community that was thriving. A result of his conscious choice to change his life and do it out of love.

Terve's yields were larger than the rest of the farmers in the area. His soil was richer, and the produce tasted the best, too. Vendors inundated him with requests. He was building a reputation that extended beyond the community. Because Terve's success was not typical nor his crop yields normal, local farmers catching wind of his success began consulting with him about his efforts. They were just nosey to find out how such a novice was so successful.

He looked out the kitchen window, excited about the day ahead. It was the anniversary of planting Teija's ashes in the forest. To commemorate the day, he planned a picnic with the kids in the forest at their sanctuary for Teija. Later, a few friends and family were coming over for dinner. He wanted to thank Sarah, Philip, Ryan, and his parents for their support.

Since the stables were complete, Terve had added horses to their family. The children were amazing riders. Each one was eagerly responsible for his horse; an agreement they struck with Terve to have horses.

He loaded up the packs on the horses and asked the kids to gather up anything else they wanted to bring with them. The farm store stand had a sign on it:

"Closed for today. Going to visit Mom."

Kali left the note there. Everyone in town knew their mother passed so he figured it was fine.

Terve encouraged the children to talk to and about Teija whenever they wanted. He led by example and made sure he always talked to her out loud around them. He kept pictures of her in their bedrooms and made no excuses when they caught him talking to her, unaware of their presence. Of course, he kept some things private and shared those when he would visit the site alone. Today, he was especially excited to share with her his success on the farm. The kids made homemade cards and painted rocks last night at the table with his mother's help to deliver to Teija's grave.

Sky wide open blue and bright. Paintbrush strokes of white clouds paint the sky. It's the best day to visit her, Terve thinks. They pass the Aspens and Terve raises his hand and signals to Veli as the kids ride by. Kaia asks her dad, "What are you doing with your hands, Dad?"

He responds, "I am just greeting the forest, sweetheart."

"Why?"

"Because the Aspens are friends to us. They watch over the forest and our land. It would be rude not to greet them."

"I don't understand."

"It's like when you visit Grandma's house. You wouldn't walk in the house and not speak to her."

"I guess not."

"I am just doing the same thing. We are entering the forest's house, so to speak."

The children knew that their dad had conversations in abstract ways and that his tattoos were not like other peoples, but they just chalked that up to be their dad and didn't understand his significance. They were innocent children who love their father and that was enough for now.

As if sensing his arrival, hummingbirds followed them to the magical site they had grown so fond of during this first year. They had camped and made s'mores and told ghost stories here. Terve visited her alone, often when he wanted to clear his head or seek guidance. They always brought flowers or other gifts for Teija. For Mother's Day, they brought a wind chime to hang on the trees. He wanted the twins to have the gift of remembering her and never feeling bad about it. When he felt comfortable with the twins riding skills, he'd let them ride out to visit her without him as long as they carried their cell phones.

Terve leading, the three round the corner where he tells his horse, Rohkea, to halt. Standing in the center of the site where he had placed the remembrance placard stood a tree. A fully grown tree. They all dismount their horses and stand still for a long time. The tree looked odd like the wind turned it inside out like an umbrella in a storm. It did not match any of the other trees around. The branches and limbs looked like roots growing in the wrong direction. The leaves shimmered and glistened with little white and yellow flowers opening and closing slowly at the top. As if queued up for their arrival, all the wildflower packets they planted encircling their mother's ashes bloomed for their visit.

"Dad, where did this tree come from?"

"Did you and Uncle Philip plant this for the anniversary?" the twins asked in unison.

Terve, still stunned, says, "What the hell?!"

Kali quickly corrects him. "Dad! Language!"

Rohkea, sensing something is off, saunters up closer to Terve and nudges him to remind him that he is nearby.

"Easy boy!" Terve pats his side with authority to let him know all is well.

"Can we go see it?" Kaia asks him.

Terve, still unsure of what is happening, asks them to just give him a second. During the shock and awe, he missed the butterflies flying near him, the faint humming noise in his left ear, and the energy coursing through his palms. Terve knew instinctively that this tree was different, though not harmful. Terve did not yet understand its reason for being.

"Why don't we all walk together to a seat on one of the rocks and rest here for a while."

Terve looks long and hard at the mysterious tree. Mysterious because it wasn't there last week when he came out for his usual visit. It is like the tree arrived just in time for the anniversary. How could the tree even know about Teija? Bewildered, he takes a deep breath in and out and looks around for confirmation or clarity. Terve begins a conversation with himself inside his head.

"Wait is this what was in the packets?"

"I planted those seeds a year ago and nothing ever grew in the spot."

"What kind of seed takes a year to germinate?"

"What kind of seed does all of its growth in one week?"

"Dad," Kali says.

"Dad, can we touch the tree yet?"

Still unsure of its origin he takes a picture of it for later. He wants to ask Ryan, the landscaper, at dinner tonight if he knows anything about it.

"Sure, kids, but be careful."

The children pull out their cards for their mother's grave along with the fresh flowers and painted rocks. Placing the items carefully near the foot of the tree, each twin wishes their mom a happy anniversary. Terve spreads out a blanket off to the side and unpacks the horses to set up lunch. He remembers the first time he found this site. The circle of rocks fascinated him, and he felt like this place was probably used before his arrival. Over the past twelve months its truly been a gift to come out here and unload so he could return refreshed for his children.

After lunch, the kids ask if they can ride on their own for a while and meet him back at the house. He realizes that they are no longer children. They are growing up and soon will want lives of their own. Their independence scares him. He is not ready to be alone on the farm nor let them go.

"Sure, but don't forget we are hosting dinner tonight. I'll need your help with the cooking and preparations."

Before he can finish the last few words, the twins are already on their horses, headed out of the haven.

He sits alone and lowers his head in his hands. Running his fingers through his hair, he looks up at the tree and begins to talk to Teija:

"They'll be going off to college before you know it. I wish you were here to see them. Kaia is so much like you. She has become quite the beekeeper. She likes to hang around Sarah and help her with the honey. I think she likes having a woman around to talk to. She is sort of outnumbered by us guys."

Terve smiles and chuckles as if Teija were sitting right there. He tells her about the tree's sudden appearance and about the seeds he planted a year ago. He lingers on, telling her about Kali and how his riding skills outmatch his own and how he is enjoying watching him grow into a man. He asks her about tonight's menu and what she thinks. As if she is responding, he nods his head.

"Ok, I've got to get back and get ready for our guest. I will see you in a few days," he promises.

Terve kisses his fingertips and presses them to the earth near the placard they placed last year. He pauses briefly and says a few more words privately to Teija before mounting Rohkea for the ride home.

"Let's go, boy."

Terve rides slowly back home. He breathes deeply and blows out a loud breath and does it again. A practice he does when he wants to control his emotions. He looks over the land and the farm and he remembers the day he drove with Ryan to the forest to show him the location where he wanted to create a refuge.

It was that same day that he saw the mirage of the Greenhouse on his property. With the arrival of the tree, he decided that the seeds must be seeds from the tree. He makes a mental note to talk to Philip at dinner. He is going to build a greenhouse and plant the remainder of Reya's seeds inside it. He had wanted a safe place to plant the seeds she left behind. He felt their survival was necessary, and he wanted to give them the best chance possible to grow. He rationalized the expense by telling himself he could use some of the space to grow the local vendors' requests along with herbs. Herbs were one thing he hadn't dabbled in yet. This would be an opportunity to stretch his abilities. He thought that the money he received from the vendors would pay for the Greenhouse and starting Reya's seeds.

"That's a win-win," he tells himself.

With renewed excitement about the coming days, Terve gives Rohkea a "Giddy up!" and gallops the rest of the way home.

CHAPTER 16
THE FARM

S ince the anniversary dinner five years ago, Terve has accomplished a lot. He starts most days alone in the Greenhouse. He gets up earlier than the twins to have this time alone with the plants. He spends these moments enjoying the feelings he accesses in the Greenhouse while he sips his coffee. Each day, pausing at the doorway to the Greenhouse, he feels his anticipation rise. He never knows from day to day how he will feel or what he might learn inside. Sometimes, though, just as he touches the door handle, an inkling bubbles up or a question arises that he'd like to explore that day. Terve tells the twins that each time he opens the door, he hears a sigh or aww sound; like the Greenhouse was waiting for him to return. He enters the space and breathes deeply and then lets his intuition flow. It's different than the farm outside. The farm has a strong sense of connection and understanding. He feels like he accesses a network that lies even deeper than the seeds buried there. But in the Greenhouse, he feels awkward like a newcomer. He is unsure sometimes about the feelings he gets so he pulls out Reya's notes and starts combing through them again.

Now, in addition to his coffee and his quiet moments alone, he adds notes to Reya's book. He finds that her descriptions of plants are more intimate. It feels like she is describing a lover or a person, not a plant. Terve's experience with them was different. He sensed the needs of the plants. He could feel when the soil needed acid or alkaline nutrients. He could feel the water content and determine if he needed to adjust sprinklers. It felt like Terve was accessing the physical needs of the plant and paying closer attention to them because of the notes Reya made. She seems to have felt the essence of the plants and he sensed the combination of both insights might prove valuable down the line somewhere. He was unsure how or why, but he was fascinated enough to continue. Reya, it appeared, drew a correlation to the plants' essence and the symbols they ignited in her. Terve always felt his link to the symbols came from his heart talking to the plants. He decided to try to discern which one it was or whether it was a combination of both.

Most mornings his exploration began by standing as still as possible in the center of the Greenhouse, waiting for the movements in his body to begin. Sometimes his knowing would pull him to a specific area in the Greenhouse or to one plant. He might find himself standing in front of a group of petunias and feel his hands shimmy a little. He might taste acid in his mouth or feel prickling feelings on his skin. These clues, he'd call them, would trigger further investigation of the health and wellbeing of the plant. If the plant had an infestation of an insect, he'd feel a crawling sensation on his hands. If the plants had too much water, he'd feel like he needed to swallow a mouthful of water. Sometimes, however, he was drawn to flowering feverfew without any physical sensation. He would sit and wait and wait and then he would feel a subtle shift around him, and he'd feel drawn in closer to the plant. The feverfew would transfer information about itself to Terve but without words. For example, he might sense that the feverfew was awakening a small spot in his heart for lovingkindness or delightful play. These Moments are when he felt like he was getting a sense of what Reya felt. And no surprise that these happenings occurred around plants born out of Reya's seeds. The information seemed abstract and without direction and difficult for him to relate to, but he would record it anyway. He thought perhaps if there was a Reya out there before him, there might be someone else like them that could decipher these meanings. So Terve approached his work like a scientist without judgement or expected outcomes and just observed and documented. The more he did, the more he felt tuned-in to the plants and the land outside the Greenhouse.

Although the seeds Reya buried in the fields never produced plants, Terve sensed that the little graves she created in his fields are what nurtures the land and connects the crops to an unknown source of energy that flows through this special place.

Expansion during those five years gave rise to myriad projects. He grew herbs and heirloom vegetables along with other vendor requests in the Greenhouse. With advanced technology, Terve could set temperatures inside allowing him to keep some items year-round, regardless of the weather.

He took advantage of the space and put it to good use. Reya's seeds were one of the first things he planted. He thought that little dragon blood trees would sprout from the seeds, but he was wrong. To date, not one envelope produced a dragon blood tree. Most of the seeds grew into ordinary things you might find in any nursery or farm. Some packets were peppers while others were wild daisies.

The truth was, Terve never knew what was going to sprout when he covered the seeds with the soil. He decided it didn't matter. What mattered was the result. More people started visiting the farm. He expanded the farm cart to a full-blown store where he sold everything grown on the farm. He also allowed other farmers to feature items in the store, spreading the network within his community.

With interest in the farm peaking, Terve, with Kaia's help, created a blog about the farm. He shared the story of the seeds with the town and when one of Reya's seeds bloomed or sprouted a new tomato or flower, he invited the community out to visit. When another farmer wanted to feature something in the farm store, he'd put a note about it on the blog to let everyone know about the availability. Terve would hold virtual raffles for items found in the store, too. Sometimes, when one of Reya's seeds grew, he would raffle it off and send it home with a member of the community. The only catch was that any seeds produced by the plant be carefully returned to the farm so that it could be replanted in the Greenhouse. Although he enjoyed planting the mysterious seeds without knowing what would grow. He asked that when they returned the seeds that they be placed in labeled envelops. Terve didn't mind if they kept a few seeds for their gardens, but he wanted to ensure the continuation of the special seeds.

All funds raised from the raffles were donated to Sarah's bee conservation efforts that supported bee hotel production and delivery along with tutorials about bee management. He encouraged the community to join their blog to share stories and pictures of their journey with Reya's plants. The blog was a success, but not the way you might think. Sure, people took pictures and updated Terve about their plants, and, as promised, they returned envelopes of seeds with one exception: labels. Whenever someone would take home a plant, their life would shift somehow. They would decide to go back to school, make amends with an estranged family member, or just find that their day to day was filled with more joy. The blog became a conduit for connection with the Greenhouse as the catalyst. The community was evolving emotionally together because of their appreciation and gratitude for the plants and the bees.

The blog also opened the conversation about Terve and his understandings and discoveries about the plants. Finally, the tattoos on his arm were discussed. Others who had witnessed him in the fields making funny gestures started talking about it on the blog. Terve, sensing he needed to say something, posted the following:

The mysterious tattoos: I've had the markings on my arms since I was a little boy. I've never really known where they come from or why, but I have always known that I have a sensitivity to nature as a result. I sense the plants and their needs. No, I'm not talking to the plants like a crazy person. The communication comes from a place unknown. The hand gestures you see me do, I believe, are gestures that fill the space and farm with love. I don't intentionally stand in the fields and do them. I stand in the fields and feel them coming and then I do them. In the past few years, I have been trying to draw a correlation between them and the crops. I have been taking notes and writing my observations. I am happy to share this with any of you who want to participate. This Saturday at noon if anyone would like to join me at the farm for a discussion, Kaia promises to make some peach scones and apple blossom iced tea. Sincerely, Terve.

Kaia attaches a "Plan to attend" button to her father's post and tracks the responses. Turns out 22 people wanted to come on Saturday. Kaia asked Sarah, the beekeeper, if she would help her prepare the scones. She had thought maybe one or two people would plan to stop by, not 22!

She told Sarah, "We are going to need a lot of scones and tea for this gig."

Sarah, laughing, "I think you are right. I know just the thing. I will bring some brambleberry and hawthorn honey to go with them."

"That sounds amazing, Sarah."

Besides the Greenhouse and the blog, Terve received calls

from local gardeners and nurseries for consultations. He would drive out to a neighboring garden or nursery and sit down for a chat. Sometimes the questions were regarding soil or why the fertilizer they purchased wasn't working. At nurseries, Terve might be asked to assess a group of young trees that were not responding well to their new environment or prematurely shedding their leaves.

No matter how large or small the problem, Terve's approach was simple: he always stood facing the plant and waited for information. Without any explanation, an outsider might be confused or find this process disturbing. Initially, some members from their town judged Terve's approach, but that was harder to do after seeing positive results. Terve never charged for any of his visits. He instead asked for their candid observations. He genuinely wanted to know the results, and what effects, if any, his visit had on their problem. Also, he did accept any and all baked pies, cakes, and casseroles to take home to the kids.

A proud father, Terve always told his clients about how responsible and brilliant his children were, and how they were eating him out of house and home. Afterward, he would laugh, sharing his enthusiasm for Kali and Kaia's accomplishments. He was rewarded with fresh beverages and multilayered conversations about his neighbor's challenges and successes. Terve felt a sense of awe that his community entrusted to him such sacred tidbits of love and life and that they all were rooted in his connection to Reya and the seeds she left to him, as well as the symbols they shared. He felt his heart opening differently during the passing years. He felt more upright and present. The overflow of energy didn't come from hubris or intellect, but from humble acknowledgements that he, too, couldn't explain.

Now, after many visits and various discussions, Terve's blog left the borders of his small community and began reaching out to others around the nation. The subtle mention of his blog from one family member to another created a force behind it. Comments multiplied exponentially along with questions. At night, Terve found himself answering questions from people he had never met. Visitors to the farm store increased; always ending with inquiries about the farmer who communes with crops.

When Saturday afternoon at the farm came, the 22 people who RSVP'd to the event arrived on time, but so did another 20 or so. Kaia and Sarah were worried, they only prepared enough food for the RSVPs. Terve, a quiet man, felt overwhelmed. He had had no intention of the event becoming a big deal. He just thought it would be a nice way to open a discussion with his neighbors about the plants and the farm. Philip came to offer moral support and Terve was grateful. Kali came out of the stables to help people park their cars and Philip skillfully informed the individuals who invited themselves that they would have to stand in the back behind those who had made reservations.

"Now what do I do?" Terve asks Philip. "This was supposed to be a casual talk, not an assembly."

Terve looks out at the group before him and steps forward to talk. He thanks them all for coming out and genuinely expresses how unexpected the massive turnout was. He told them his true intention was just to talk about the farm and answer questions, but also perhaps to explore the observations he was making in the Greenhouse.

He shared a little about Reya and the land and the way it looked when he first saw it. He shared with them about his experience in the oak tree and how he got his tattoos. He suspected many of them didn't believe him; he was used to that. Then he told them something that none of them expected. He told them that he sensed a change in some of his crops. He mentioned that sense was reinforced recently with his local visits to other growers. One of the locals ask him what it was he sensed. He told her that he wasn't quite sure, but he felt that something was changing on a cellular level and he didn't understand it, but the impact may not be positive. He didn't want to alarm anyone, so he disguised his observation as a call for help. He asked all of them to monitor their gardens and trees closely along with the bees and use the blog to share any insights. He humbly suggested the event was a community effort, not his alone, and that if they were to continue holding these events, something he thought useful, others should step forward and host them, too.

Terve talked a little more and then closed the meeting. He encouraged everyone to stay and talk and share and of course have some iced tea and a scone while they lasted.

While everyone slowly mingled and dispersed, a woman approached Terve and asked if she could talk to him.

She introduced herself, "Hi, I'm Doctor Laura Lemmon."

Terve looked at her intently and responded. "Pleased to meet you, Laura."

"What can I do for you?" he asked.

"If it is ok, Mr. Summer, I'd like to talk to you more about your work here. My research at the University is about stress on our bio networks and how that is affecting plants. Specifically, I'm tasked to look at increasing reports of oxidative stress in multiple systems."

Terve, dumbfounded just looked at her for a long pause and said,

"First, call me Terve, and second, I have no idea what you are talking about, but it sounds important."

She chuckled. His candor was disarming and attractive. "I'm sorry. I have a habit of doing that."

"Doing what?" he asks.

"Rambling without providing any context."

Now it was Terve who was smiling, "Yeah, I get that."

Laura told him that when he expressed a sense that the

plants were changing, it piqued her curiosity. She thought perhaps he was sensing what she had discovered through research. She suggested they could compare their work to consider if there were any overlaps. Open to the possibility, Terve asked her to coordinate a time to meet and discuss in depth. Laura asked if he might come to the university so she could show him instead. Terve, never wanting to be far from the farm or his children told her he would consider it.

"I'll call you, mid-week to set up something, okay?" she asks.

Terve responds. "Look forward to it."

Terve felt a shiver when Laura left. One he had not felt before and one that did not fascinate him but rather concerned him.

CHAPTER 17
DÉJÀ VU

G ood as her word, Laura called Terve mid-week and asked him to visit her at the university. Wednesday morning, he woke up early as usual and headed to his outdoor sanctuary, the shower. As he leaned into the soothing water, he decided to wash his body, and especially his hands, with a body scrub that one of the locals started selling in the farm store. Farming was a dirty business, literally. He loved the feeling of the soil in his hands and never minded getting his feet and hands dirty, but he didn't want to wear it, nor did he want it taking up real estate under his fingernails or toes. The scrub smelled of honey, maple and pecans with a bit of a rosemary afterthought. The scent was so enticing, he scrubbed harder to work the essential oils up to create a mesmerizing sensory escape. Immediately, he thought of Reya and the notes about different mixtures she recorded for scrubs and oils. He quickly looked at the container to see who made the scrub. "Bee Clean" was listed on the container. He saw Sarah's name. Surprised, he didn't know Sarah did anything else but honey. He made a mental note to tell her how much he enjoyed the scrub the next time he saw her.

Terve dressed, grabbed toast and coffee, and headed out to the stables to talk to Rohkea. He fed him an apple and blew into his nostrils a little. Mentally, he stood there reworking his normal daily checklist to include visiting the university. He texted Kali, asking him to take care of Rohkea today.

Terve glanced over his shoulder and looked toward the Greenhouse and saw a shift in the space around it. It was quick and he wasn't sure if it was just fatigue in his eyes, but he thought he saw movement in the area surrounding it.

When Terve arrived at the university, he had a flash of *déjà vu*. He walked slowly toward the Margaret Eastwood building to find Dr. Lemmon. Her office was on the second floor, so he decided to take the stairs.

TULEVAISUUS RAISES HIS HAND AND SCRATCHES HIS HEAD. HIS ELBOW JABS LASNA WHO LOOKS BACK, PERTURBED.

As he entered the second-floor hallway, Terve paused to look at the wall placard with names and room numbers, searching for Dr. Lemmon. He didn't recall if she mentioned her office number. The halls were bright and filled, not surprisingly, with pictures of plants and their life cycles along with famous scientists he assumed made contributions to botany. He also noticed pictures of land, farms, and aerial photos of locations unfamiliar to him.

Distracted by the overflow of visual stimuli, he stopped to look at each of the photos on the wall. He approached a photo of a building and the Moment he looked at the picture he felt himself drift into a somewhere else. In front of him, it looked like he was in the same place, but the desks and layouts were different. Blinking several times, he couldn't feel his efforts making a difference. He saw a man walking down toward him, calling for someone.

"Nu, where are you?" Terve watched the man approach a little girl standing in front of a picture just like he was.

She was pointing up to the picture, telling her father, "That's the boy in the oak tree, Daddy. Can I go play with him?"

Terve tried to move closer to see the picture the little girl was pointing to, but his body was frozen. He watched the man pick up the child and walk right by him. Neither one sees him, but he notices the child's skin looks like his, but her markings are part of her skin not on top like his. Just as they pass him, the girl's skin lights up. He knows they must be connected because her symbols recognized him. He knows what he is seeing is real, but he doesn't know how or when or why.

Unable to move, he stands there waiting for his body and mind and spirit to merge again so he can feel himself whole. As he slowly feels movement in his toes, he hears a voice and looks to see if the man and little girl are returning.

"Glad to see you made it, Terve," Laura says.

"Dr. Lemmon!" Startled, Terve greets Laura louder than his normally calm demeanor.

"Is everything all right? I didn't mean to startle you," Laura replies. She extends her hand to offer support. Terve's pupils are dilated and his footing unsure. He looks at Laura like he is looking through her. She gently touches his arm and asks him again if he is all right. The second time, he realizes he is still not fully present. Mind racing, he doesn't know this person well enough to share these happenings with her. So Terve internally tries to snap himself back into his body. To buy himself some time he asks her for some water. Laura leads him to her office, room 2112.

"Have a seat while I get you a bottle of water."

Laura walks the opposite way, and he sinks into her chair attempting to categorize what took place. "Just breathe man," he tells himself. "Just breathe!!"

Terve takes a second and focuses on the honey, maple, and rosemary scrub he used this morning and tries to feel himself back into this reality. Feeling centered again, he looks around her office for clues. He is curious about her and what she may want to show him. Her desk is scattered with multiple binders and presentations. Snooping through them a little, he looks at some of the titles but doesn't understand what they mean. If she has a system for filing, it is not apparent. Tucked between two binders is a half-eaten sandwich along with a handful of grapes. He is unsure of how old it is. Eating appears to be an afterthought. Suddenly, he wants to feed her. Shocked by that thought, he clears his throat and continues taking inventory of this mystery woman.

She has multiple cups of different beverages scattered about, too. One looks like coffee, the other is iced tea, and the third looks like some concoction that he would not even consider drinking. He speculates whether it is an experiment and not a drink at all. He also feels pride and fascination in the office. It feels different than the "hum" he feels in the fields. It feels more like an "Aww." Her walls are covered with pictures and diagrams of plants, except for one. On that is a picture depicting the pollination process and the integral role bees and other pollinators play for so many plants. His heart feels happy seeing the bees on the wall. As he sits back in the chair and relaxes a little, Laura returns and offers him the water.

Terve takes the water and swallows it all in one gulp. He doesn't realize that until he sees the startled look on Laura's face.

He decides instead of explaining himself to just push through to the conversation she invited him here for.

"Thanks," he says. "Why don't you show me what you wanted me to see?"

"Mr. Summer . . ."

"Please, Terve," he interrupts.

"Sorry, Terve, I brought you here to look at some of my findings. Our team is studying the collapse and failure of biodiversity. We see evidence of this in various ways. Bee colonies are dying out at astronomical levels. They are showing signs of malformation in their wings that make them more vulnerable to attack. We are also witnessing mites attacking them. The mites we are witnessing are not even supposed to be in the United States. They are sucking the life out of the bees and we have yet to find a way to kill them off without harming the bees. The bees as you know from farming are integral to the pollination of cash crops, as well as fruits and vegetables. We are also seeing increases in phytotoxicity in plants."

"Photo what?" Terve asks.

"Phytotoxicity," Laura repeats.

"I understand very little right now about what you are saying but I can feel it's important. Is there any way to simplify this for me?"

She looks at him, frustrated, then continues, "To put it bluntly, we are seeing poor germination, death of seeds and succulent tissue, stunted growth, and necrosis in plants and crops. They are dying at a rate that may lead to extinction of fruit and vegetable species. Have you identified the cause? He asks.

"With global populations continuing to rise, the need for food increased. With the fear of running out of food, farmers working with scientists looked for ways to secure crops and create consistency in yields. You know their efforts as commercialized farming. Large acreage growing the same thing year after year. Now instead of small farms scattered across the world you find large corporate machines governing the growing process. Smaller farmers like yours growing the same crops are edged out all together because they cannot compete financially. We believe that in their efforts to create consistency they are in fact harming the biodiversity. "Do you understand Terve?" The solution seems to be part of the overall problem. We are destroying the balance of nature by commercial farming, commercial livestock, and deforestation in efforts to make room for the ever-growing population. It is not just us. Do you see all these binders and papers? They are projects from other scientists, and we are all coming to similar conclusions."

"What!!!" Terve leans forward with the deepest concern.

"You see," she says, "plants have natural defenses but those defenses, when bombarded with changes in the biodiversity, can lead to overload and destruction. Changes in climate, soil, and pathogens can all trigger oxidative stress in plants."

"Okay," he leans back, "you lost me again."

Laura smiles as she passes him a binder and asks if he'll take it home and look at it.

"Have you noticed any changes in your crop yields or your hives?"

Terve looked at her calmly and said "No. I also haven't felt any shifts in the way the fields feel. I have however sensed something is off, but I haven't identified what yet."

Laura looks at him with skepticism. "What do you mean when you say you haven't felt any?"

Terve looks at her and his arms start to tingle. He tells her about his connection to the field, the plants, and the Green-house. Terve shares with her the vulnerability in the soil that he senses when it isn't right or when the water levels or other inputs need to be changed.

"I also believe that the land I live on is truly special, and it energetically holds a true connection to something unknown but vital. A vital force that is unimaginable to our minds runs below the surface of my farm."

Laura's response is direct and rather cool, "Your explanation, although poetic, isn't in a context that I can relate to. My source is not experience but solid research."

Terve looks at her, saddened but not surprised.

Spontaneously he says, "Well, now you know how I felt minutes ago when you were trying to scientifically explain to me your findings."

"Touché," she says.

Laura goes on to tell him that she took a Moment to look at his blog and noticed some of the conversations he was sharing about plants.

"If these blog inputs are true, then perhaps you can help me. Help me understand in your language what is happening. More importantly, do you believe that this is a way to reverse the damage and perhaps save our way of life?"

As Terve looks at Laura, she changes into a ferocious lioness. She is impassioned and afraid. Like a lioness protecting her cubs, Laura wants to protect the plants and the farmers' way of life. Terve realizes the feeling he got from her back at the farm was fear. He sees the desperation in the depth of her right eye (The eye Terve looks at when he wants to evaluate someone's emotional state.) that wasn't there upon his initial glance or at least he didn't notice it. It looks feral and raw and it is the kind of fear that you must approach skillfully. Terve knew instinctively he had to tread lightly about what came out of his mouth next.

"Do you think this phyto . . . whatever you call it, can happen on my farm?"

She stares at him and feels disarmed by his vulnerability. Her warrior goddess lays down her sword for him and moves to the chair next to him. She is self-conscious about creating too much fear in others even though she is frightened by the test results she is seeing.

"I wish I could say no, but I think it is very possible."

His ego will not allow this conversation to continue. "I can't imagine that will happen to my farm. I won't let it!" he responds with determination.

"I hope that is the case, Terve. In the meantime, I'd like to learn more about your farm and what is going on there. If I may, I'd like to visit a few more times. Perhaps I can discover something new there that others have not yet been able to find."

Terve thinks she might just be stroking his ego but at this Moment he doesn't care.

He offers, "Come out anytime you like. If you give me a heads up, I will make your lunch."

Terve looks down at the sandwich again and the rest of her desk and adds, "Looks like you could use it."

Smiling a little, she looks at her desk and realizes what he must think. Touched by his observation, she thanks him for the offer and tells him that she is happy to have someone cook for her.

"Well, it looks like I have some homework to do." He smiles tapping the binder she gave him. He stands up, shakes her hand, and tells her he looks forward to her call.

Terve takes one more look at her and then turns and walks back out the way he came with one exception: he takes the elevator instead of the stairs.

During the drive home, Terve meditates on his conversation with Laura and wonders if things are as bad as she tells him. He thinks of his children and what life they will have if what she said is true. He wonders about the little girl he saw in the hallway. Who was the little boy in the oak tree she wanted to play with? Why did the office space look and feel different, yet the same?

Terve decides he's too hungry to answer these questions now. He feels a strong desire to stand in his fields and connect. He speeds home with purpose and decisiveness. It felt to him like he was being pulled through the traffic without the normal resistance of driving. He knew something was off when he arrived home in half the time.

CHAPTER 18
UNEXPECTED GUESTS

W hen he got out of his truck, Terve walked straight to the fields without seeing anyone nor talking to anyone. He rolled up his sleeves and let the light show begin. He wanted to feel that the fields were all right for himself. He wanted to disappear into them and so he did. He held his hands up, palms out, and began pushing at the air gently waiting for the air and the waves to push back. He was waiting to be swept away in nature, but he also wanted reassurance that the farm was alive and well. The waves surrounded his hands and lifted them above his head where they came together. His thumbs and first finger made a triangle for him to look through. He held this position for a long time without his arms tiring. There is a flash and then a feeling of strength that washes over him. He feels unbreakable. He feels strong and rooted there and he feels the fear he felt in Laura's office wash away.

Slowly, his hands lower and all ten fingers begin to pulsate. As if each finger has its own heartbeat, Terve feels his hands are no longer his hands. He looks at them and they no longer look like his hands. Shocked by this revelation, he shakes his hands and his head, and the feeling disappears, but what he experienced lingers. He cannot shake it. He questions for the first time in a long time who he is.

Walking back toward the house, he notices something growing up in between the corn.

"What is that?" he thought. He walked over and saw a stem with just a handful of green leaves on it.

"A weed," he says while simultaneously plucking it.

He shakes his head because the team that works the farm with him is normally on top of weeds. Looking at the height, it must have been there for several days to be this tall. Out of the corner of his eye, Terve sees another plant a few rows over, growing up between the cabbages. He walks over, confused, and bends down again and plucks it.

"That's two in one day. I have to talk with the team and find out what is going on."

Terve accepts that weeds are part of growing food. He also knows that seeds don't choose where they land, they just do what they do and if the environment is right, they grow. He makes a mental note to walk the rest of the fields before the end of the day to ensure there isn't a problem.

Famished, and with the door wide open, he just starts grabbing things out of the refrigerator and eating them. In one hand, he is holding a brick of cheese and the other he is downing a handful of fresh grape tomatoes. Freeing up one hand from the cheese, he grabs a pickle and some onions. Laughing at himself, he sets the items on the counter, grabs a plate, and sits. Terve grabs some dill and peppercorns and grinds them in a mortar and pestle. Afterward, he throws in some mayo and dark mustard and creates his own aioli. He slowly butters a soft brioche bun, then toasts it on the griddle. Once the toasted side is golden, he removes it from the griddle and generously spreads on the aioli, making a sandwich. He slices the sandwich in half and thinks of Laura.

Shocked that he is thinking of any woman, let alone

someone who is so different from him, he wonders if she might like the sandwich and decides that maybe he'll make it for lunch when she comes. Terve takes a few sips of his IPA and looks out the window toward the fields and the Greenhouse. The cool beer quenches his thirst and heightens the taste of the cheddar cheese in his sandwich. The sandwich hit the right spot in his stomach.

He feels grateful for the freshness that surrounds him as a farmer. He enjoys the richness that the soil infuses in his food. He feels his body acknowledge the organic vibrancy and honors what this space provides him, his children, and his community. He feels pride, but he also feels connected. He feels connected to the earth and the people and the mountains that watch over them. He feels enriched by invisible things and cannot do it justice with words. Terve grasps that in this Moment he is describing happiness. He isn't sure that he has allowed himself to even think that since his wife died. Looking out at all of it, he decides he feels happy and for several reasons and no reasons and that the absolutely remarkable observation of it also makes him happy. He sighs and smiles for the first time in years from the inside out.

Later that night, Terve dreams:

He feels hot. The temperature is overwhelming, and he feels the sweat on his body. He sees dirt and dust in places inhabited by green plush crops before. He tastes a bitter metal taste in his mouth and tries to spit it out but cannot. The more he spits the stronger the taste of metal. As he swallows his mouth fills again with a salty taste followed by petroleum. He hovers his hand over the dirt, but his hands and body do not respond. He feels the heavy stench of death weighing down the air around him. Laying on the ground all around his feet are thousands of bee hotels. Dead bees lay sprawled outside of them as if seeking refuge but not making it in time. He looks beyond the fields and sees people packing and leaving their homes. He can't get to them to ask them where they are going because his feet will not move. The sun feels like its hovering just above his head. It feels oppressive and he wants to escape and yet his feet will still not move. Suddenly, Terve sees the mother tree, Aiti, floating upward toward the sky. She is surrounded by the trees he planted for his wife's memorial. The sky changes from blue to purple and he waves to Aiti, but she does not see him.

She is floating out of his grasp and he yells to her. "Come back! Please, come back!"

He falls to the ground and grabs at a small square of grass that remains. The grass is a life he can feel as he crawls sorrowfully. Suddenly, a weed sprouts up among the living blades of grass. Terve is angry seeing it there. He attempts to pull it out as he did earlier in the field, but it will not budge. He puts all his strength into it but the little green leaves thriving amongst the sea of death that surrounds him still won't budge. With his skin on fire, Terve is screaming to pull out the plant. The pain from the heat unbearable, he wakes up screaming.

Terve jumps out of bed and hurries toward the shower. His body is on fire and he needs to cool down. He doesn't wait to test the temperature; he just turns the shower knob and walks into his sanctuary. He doesn't bother to adjust the handle; he leaves it on cold until he is shaking. It is the shaking that finally relieves him from the pain of his dream. He repeats over and over,

"It was just a dream."

"It was just a dream."

"It was just a dream."

But deep inside it didn't feel like a dream, it felt real, it felt true, and it terrified him.

Terve's remaining hours before dawn were restless. He didn't want to fall asleep and risk revisiting the same dream. He hated to admit it, but he felt afraid. A childlike fear like when you believe monsters are living under your bed or you swear you see something alive in your closet and call out for your mother to save you.

Terve thought of calling Nea but felt silly. He decided

instead to thumb through the pages of the binder Laura gave him. The scientific jargon was difficult for him to follow. He studied biology and chemistry in college, but that was years ago. He decided to stick with the abstract and summary overviews instead. After several hours of Googling words and phrases, Terve got the gist of what she was trying to tell him. He had questions, of course, and he would ask them when he saw her, but he sensed that the dream was a foreshadowing. He paused to think that the amazing Moment he experienced in his kitchen earlier might all be swept away by a problem of our own doing.

Realizing he wasn't going back to sleep, Terve decides to take another shower, this one for pleasure. He grabs for his razor and decides to shave first. While he stands in front of the mirror shaving his face, he feels his fingertips tingle. They are drawn to the mirror. Terve takes a second and allows his fingers to move closer. Close enough to touch the mirror but hovering near the glass instead. He feels the pulsation engorge his fingertips with blood. He leans in for a closer look and his eyes look back at him. They are his eyes, but also, they are not. They look at him with an intensity that he can only relate to as a feeling, not an expression. He doesn't recall ever seeing such force behind his eyes. The force scares him and also invigorates him somehow. He shakes his head and snaps back to shaving, but secretly keeps staring at his eyes to see if that "look" returns.

For the third time in less than 24 hours, Terve steps inside the sanctuary again and reaches for the shower gel that his daughter Kaia developed, working with Sarah in the Greenhouse. Supporting her brilliance, he offered to try it out. She is so excited that he is willing to participate. She told him that she's calling the line *Spa Boy*. It's going to be a line of body products just for men. She plans to create a new shampoo and conditioner, too. He loves his daughter's creativity and promises he will let her know what he thinks.

Terve reaches for the gel and pushes down on the plunger. The fragrance of patchouli with peppermint fills the shower. The combination is surprisingly earthy but simultaneously airy, too. He feels grounded and lighthearted. He lathers up a few times, enjoying the sensation of the peppermint while relaxing into the patchouli.

"Well done, Kaia. Your mother would be so proud."

She would be proud of the twins. Kali has taken over the stables and will head off to veterinarian school in the fall. Kaia is opting to pursue a degree in phytology with an emphasis on conservation, a choice Terve feels was heavily influenced by Sarah's work. He reminds himself to remind them how much their mother would have loved to see them thriving.

Since he's up earlier than normal, Terve decides to spend extra time in the kitchen making breakfast. Normally, the kids, who aren't kids anymore, help themselves to breakfast before rushing off to school. He thought they might be compelled to sit down with him if the breakfast was outrageous. Terve pulled out all the stops for this breakfast. The dream made him want to celebrate the "NOW." He wanted to give them abundance while he could for as long as he could. Even if they didn't understand why, he wanted to pour his heart into the food so it might surround them like a protective blanket. An assortment of waffles, fresh fruit, sausage, eggs, biscuits, with fresh butter and hot maple syrup, covered every inch of the breakfast table.

Terve stands at the head of the table and calls Kali and Kaia down for breakfast. Sarah, who was out tending the hives, has been invited to join them. The kids distracted in their self-absorption, were irritated by their father's calls, but came downstairs anyway. Both looked at each other and then back at their father with shock. They haven't seen a feast like this on a weekday since their mother passed.

Immediately, shock turned to apprehension and Kali breaks

the silence with, "Who died?" Kaia punches his arm and tells her brother to shut up.

Kaia tentatively looks at her dad and asks, "Is something wrong, Dad?"

"No."

"What's with the huge breakfast then, on a school day?"

"I just wanted you guys to have a special breakfast."

"But why? What is so special about a Tuesday?"

Gently stroking his daughter's head, he looks at her and says, "You are! So is that powerful shower gel you made."

"Dad, seriously, what's wrong? You are being weird."

"No, I'm not. I just wanted you two to know how much I love you."

Kali looks at his sister and then back as his father. "Seriously, who died?"

"Stop saying that! Nobody died! Just sit down and eat breakfast with me."

Sarah taps on the door and walks in. "Wow! Look at this spread. What's the occasion?"

Kali looks at Sarah sarcastically and says, "Dad is losing it. You need to keep an eye on him today while we're at school."

Sarah looks at Terve, searching for any sign of illness, mental or otherwise. He looks back at her like, "Not you, too?"

She smiles at him with a curiosity and then sits down with everyone else. To break the ice, she looks back at the twins and says, "Well, if this is the result, let's hope he decides to lose it a little more often!"

Kaia and Kali crack up laughing, and they all dig into the feast.

Terve watches his family eat with passion and his heart feels a sense of accomplishment, but also realizes that their response to his efforts was telling. His children believe they must have a reason to celebrate or indulge or be outrageous. He didn't want that for them. He didn't want his children to question their worthiness to abundance and the expression of it. He also didn't want them to wait to celebrate their lives. He wanted them to embrace their opportunities when they were presented. It is something he realized he could work on. At that Moment, Terve committed to having more breakfasts like this one. To celebrate more often "just because," and to permit the twins to do the same.

Once he has the house to himself, Terve takes a few Moments to go over his daily checklist and sip some hot coffee. The dream creeps back in his periphery and he recalls the weeds from the prior day. He must walk the fields and look for more. He also can't shake the weed in his dream that he couldn't pull out. He was searching for meaning. Why was it so difficult to pull out in the dream when it was easy in the fields? Maybe the weed represents something in his life he needs to get rid of but can't. He scratches his head and thinks that he's gone too far with the psychoanalysis.

Terve decides instead to do a bit on the blog and also answer some questions. He purposefully scans for any questions about problems with people's crops or bees, but thankfully doesn't find any. However, there are more entries about Reya's plants. There is a handful of questions about the next raffle. He also notices a trend that the comments aren't just from locals. It seems Reya's plants are garnering a following, something he admittedly hadn't foreseen. Although in hindsight, the farm store started selling individual packets of the seeds once quantities allowed. He made a note to pull a report to see how many of the seed packets were sold last quarter.

@herbalgirl1 writes: "Ever since I purchased one of Reya's plants, my house is buzzing at night. I can't sleep and I am wondering if I can place it outside . . . only at night."

@spiderplantlive "The portion of seeds I kept back from Reya's plant, I put in a window box. I swear I hear wind chimes throughout

the day. Problem is, folks, I don't have a wind chime. Does anyone else have this problem?"

He doesn't spend as much time in the Greenhouse as he does the fields but decides he is going to take a look and decipher what is going on with her plants. He grabs the notebook that once belonged to Reya so he can record any observations.

Seeing no real emergent questions on the blog, nor any signs that Laura's predictions are showing up in his community, he logs off and heads outside to work. When he steps back into the field, he checks in with the soil and the plants, but still nothing. No signs of struggle or deterioration. He feels happiness and vibrancy and he is about to relax his breathing when he sees it.

It's about twenty feet in front of him. "Another one!"

What is happening he thinks? He decides that, unlike the dream, he is going to prevail and not the weed. He is about five feet away when he sees another one. The second one looks like it's in the same place as the original one was last night. He grabs his Swiss army knife from his back pocket. He wants to use the long blade to lift the little roots out ensuring it won't return. The small plant lifts out of the ground effortlessly without any resistance at all. Terve feels exonerated and strong, as if wiping out the weed will wipe away his nightmare. He turns and does the same thing to the second weed and continues walking the rest of the fields looking for more.

"Thank goodness those were the only two." Terve wipes the sweat from his brow and heads to the Greenhouse. He wants to check the health of the plants in there, too.

TULEVAISUUS WAKES UP, LOOKS ACROSS THE LAND AND CHUCKLES. HE DOES NOT INDICATE WHAT HUMORS HIM. HE LIFTS HIS ARM TO REPOSITION HIMSELF AND FALLS BACK TO SLEEP.

When Terve opens the door to the Greenhouse, he hears a young man's voice. He looks around and doesn't see anyone. The voice echoed around him. He struggles to recognize the voice. He can't place it nor where the sound came from. He just hears the young man calling out.

"If we are going to make it, we have to make the jump now."

Fascinated, Terve looks around one more time as if whoever is speaking will appear. He does not, so Terve pushes farther into the Greenhouse. He stops first and looks at some of the heirloom seeds the vendors have been growing here. The Sachet Café requested an assortment of edible flowers. They use them in salads and also recently started mixing them in homemade ice cream. The nasturtium and pansy crop looks healthy and strong, as do the tea roses. The café will be pleased.

He moves forward and looks at the Rocquencourt heirloom beans. They are coveted by Jacques, a chef whose family migrated here. He treasures these legumes and people travel from all over to eat at his tables. Terve takes a second to recognize the trust Jacques put in him. He feels touched by the courage it took for him to surrender the seeds to someone else's care.

As Terve begins to move on, he feels his arms light up and then a pull toward the row of Reya's plants. Terve walks as if a string from inside his chest pulls him forward one step at a time. All of Reya's plants are easily identified. He stands in front of them and places his right hand in front of one single seedling. The seedling pulls him closer and he leans in to look at it. He feels the space around him shift forward. It is as if the plant is pulling him out of his space and into it. The pull is strong, and he wonders how this little life has so much strength. He leans in closer yet and then it happens.

New tattoos on his arm start lighting up. The marks have

been there for as long as the others, but they have never come to life before. He wonders how he missed this. He doesn't know what these symbols mean, nor does he connect to them physically the way he does the other ones. He is startled by the possibility that the posts he read earlier might have merit. There is something to these seeds, but what? Terve remains there, looking at all of Reya's plants in a new light. He sees them from a totally new perspective.

Viime, Lasna, and Tulevaisuus are all standing up. They are looking toward the farm and watching. They are curious today about the happenings down there. They feel a shift in the surrounding area and look toward each other for acknowledgement.

CHAPTER 19
LUNCH

The following morning, Terve awakens refreshed with a feeling that the situation Dr. Lemmon described might not be that bad. As he goes about his normal routine, he feels a slight rocking in the house. He looks up at the mantle and sees the picture above it shaking ever so slightly.

"An earthquake? No, couldn't be." He brushes it off because he feels refreshed from a calm night's sleep and ready for an amazing day. Terve talks through his list as he moves toward the fields. When he finally gets out of his head and focuses, he is confounded. Not only have the two weeds returned but, at first glance, at least 80 more have sprouted overnight. This is not normal, he thinks. This is simply not possible. He has an argument with himself about the possibility of this being real. The evidence looking him in the eye might suggest otherwise. The plants have returned and with a vengeance, it would seem. He reaches for his knife, but instead pulls out his cell phone.

"Hey, Dr. Lemmon. It's Terve Summer."

"Laura, please."

"Sorry. Laura. Can you come to the farm today? There is something I need to show you."

"Is everything all right?"

"I'm not sure, but I would like to get your thoughts. I can make lunch and we can talk about the binder."

"I have a standing 11:30 conference call, but I can head out there afterward, if that is all right."

"Great! See you soon."

Terve ends the call and takes photos of the plants. He wants to save them for the blog. He needs to know if this is happening to anyone else. He also wants to ask Laura is this might be a precursor for the conditions mentioned in her research.

Laura arrives with a large briefcase that is filled with measuring devices along with vials for soil samples and high-tech imaging equipment, too. She looks like a mad scientist, Terve thinks, as he waves to her from the Greenhouse. He pauses and decides whether to share with her about Reya, her garden, or the happenings in the Greenhouse.

Laura looks excited, but also driven. She is ready to support Terve, so she dives right in. "Well, out with it. What's this situation you wanted to share with me?"

Terve walks her toward the field and points out the weed invasion.

"It happened overnight." He tells her about the two days prior with just a few weeds, but he felt this was ridiculous.

"Weeds aren't uncommon in farming, are they?"

"I know weeds aren't uncommon, but they are to us."

Terve explains to Laura his fastidious nature and how his team is trained to be the same.

"We experience weeds, but never like this, and never without warning."

"Well, let's have a look."

Laura grips a camera and walks toward the field with Terve. Her body feels excited and she is immediately self-conscious, conceding her attraction to him. She feels a strong desire to hold his hand but stops herself.

"You are a professional," she whispers to herself.

After what seems like a lifetime, Terve watches Laura walking toward him, smiling. He likes her smile and wonders what makes her happy.

"Pull yourself together, man," he chides himself. He, too, feels a little unhinged.

Laura triggers feelings in him that he packed away long ago in a box with an impenetrable lock. He smiles back as he snickers a little.

"Give it to me straight, Doc. What is happening out here?"

"Well, you don't have a weed problem. Your problem does, however, fascinate me." He looks at her perplexed.

"Those weeds aren't weeds at all. They are different types of purposeful plants. And soon, if you leave them alone, beautiful blooming plants."

He looks at her like she is speaking a different language. Perceiving his confusion, Laura tells him she can share with him more at lunch, but she wants to look around some more and take some samples. She also wants to visit the Greenhouse and check the plants that everyone talks about on his blog.

Terve feels like he is running behind and needs to catch up. She turns and heads back out and he is still stuck searching for an interpreter.

"Lunch," he thinks as he turns around and heads back inside to whip up something for Laura.

He notices he likes the way her name feels on his lips and the sound her name makes when he says it. Enchanted a bit, he decides to create something amazing for lunch.

Laura comes to the house after about an hour. The smells wafting out the front door are incredible. Quickly her stomach reminds her of her neglect. Terve welcomes her inside. He is wearing an apron, a sight she decides is handsome.

"Have a seat."

Laura sits at the big table and takes this time to look around his home. It truly does feel homey and she can feel the love in every crevice. Terve serves her a seared ahi tuna steak with a salad tossed with fresh leafy greens, chives, cilantro, and cucumbers. He drizzles fresh ginger-lime dressing over the greens. He grabs a pitcher of iced tea and some sweet rolls and adds them to the table. Impatient to hear what she has to say, Terve starts asking questions just when Laura takes the first bite of the tuna. Mouth full and embarrassed, she holds her finger up and asks for a second. Terve realizes he's out of practice in the subtleties of speaking to a woman and makes a regretful gesture. He decides to dig in as well and wait until she is ready.

Laura sees him waiting and decides to continue eating. It's too good to stop and, truthfully, she doesn't want to. She can't remember the last time, if ever, anyone cooked for her. It feels like only five minutes when Laura acknowledges she's cleaned her plate. She doesn't want to look up yet in case he is still eating.

"I think I inhaled that," she says, breaking the silence.

Her clean plate was all the thanks he needed. He liked that she ate with passion and determination. He also liked that she didn't mention that he ate quickly, too.

She pushes her plate aside and pulls the camera toward her. She opens the view screen and starts with the first picture.

"I can't be sure as to the why, although I have a theory, but I can tell you the what. This right here is not a weed. This is a *Borago officinalis*, also known as a starflower or borage plant." Laura continues, "This one is a *Hyssopus officinalis*, or hyssop plant."

"What about that one?" asked Terve.

"That one is a cosmos plant. It is part of a family of flowers like marigolds and sunflowers. These are just a few but as you witnessed, there are more out there. I'd like to study this further, if you'll allow."

"Study what?"

"It looks like the common thread I can see upon my initial observation is that all of these plants have repellant properties. For example, they can deter different types of worms, spiders, beetles, mosquitoes, and mites. For some reason unknown to me yet, these plants are strategically growing next to the vegetable or fruit that their genus of plants protects from a specific type of insect that is fond of that particular species. I know it sounds crazy and I did say it was my initial observation.

"I also visited the Greenhouse and noticed a similar trend. Whether intentional or unconsciously, it appears that Reya's plants are placed in the right space in the Greenhouse to support surrounding plants. I took several soil samples from various spots on your land to test them for the metals, salts, and toxins I spoke to you about in my office, but that will take some time for the results."

"So, you are saying I shouldn't pull them."

"I can't tell you how to run your farm, Terve, but what I can tell you is that this situation at first glance might be the answer to the questions I've been asking."

"I'm worried these 'plants,'" he says sarcastically, "might encroach on the crops and take away valuable nutrients."

"I understand your concern. Cut them back, if need be, but allow them to prosper, too, and see what happens. If you are willing, allow them to grow awhile. If I am right, your farm might be my next published work."

"That sounds great for you, but I need to ensure the livelihood of the farm."

Laura continued, "Again, this is contingent on your consent. If you let me test my hypothesis, I will include you in any decisions that might adversely affect your farm. You will have the final say. Deal?"

Terve looks at her and all he can think of is he'll get to see more of her, so he selfishly and, without regard to anyone else, agrees.

Laura excitedly jumps up and hugs him spontaneously. He stumbles back, losing his footing on impact, but recovers just in time to feel her body pressed into his. He decides he likes her close to him. He lifts his foot to move in closer just as Laura pulls away. She begins feverishly packing up her things and tells him she can't wait to get back to the university to begin drawing up the necessary paperwork. Giddy she says, "Perhaps I'll apply for a grant, too."

She heads to the door and stops. "I'm sorry. Where are my manners? Thank you for the amazing lunch and the opportunity. This is going to be big. I can feel it."

Without waiting for his response, Laura walks out the front door. This is the second time today Terve is stuck in his body and can't move, and he is frustrated by the revelation, but also disappointed that she didn't stick around longer.

CHAPTER 20

PUBLISHED REPORT #5115

L aura spent almost twelve months working on what she titled *Report #5115 The Summer Phenomena*. She spent three to four days a week out at the farm with Terve. She measured for climate effects, soil differentiation, unusual insect infestations, and crop yields. She also collected seeds from all of his crops including those in the Greenhouse. She catalogued everything they grew on the land while taking copious notes about her observations. The final report would be published later in the year, but she was already conferring with other botanists about her experiences. A handful of her peers was so curious that they made visits to the farm, too. All of them were fascinated that the farm wasn't showing any signs of soil toxicity or salinity nor were there signs of oxidative stress in the crops. The honeybee hives were thriving, producing more than average yields while other hives were dying off. A few botanists got excited when they thought that "Reya's plants" in the Greenhouse were showing subtle changes, perhaps evolutionary.

The one common mystery still unanswered was "Why?"

Laura was still not able to determine a common thread scientifically to all of these happenings.

During her work, she and Terve spent a lot more time together. They slipped into a routine. She would start early in the morning and then they'd meet for lunch at the main house. Terve even introduced her to his horses and let her ride Rohkea. During their lunches, Terve would share with Laura about Reya, her journey with the seeds, and the land here. He told her things he never told anyone before. He shared with her some of the glimpses he had and how he had a knowing about this property, that his farm would thrive here. Of course, Laura tried to understand him, but her scientific mind always wanted evidence, something she could document and record. Terve's experiences were unexplainable and the markings on his body a mystery to him, too. He, like Reya, didn't have a glossary of terms for what he felt or knew, it just came to him. He could see in Laura's eyes the desire to understand, but also the judgement that floated just behind the fascination. He'd seen it before in others he shared his gifts with, the subtly raised eyebrows or shaking heads. At the end of the day, Terve knew no one would ever understand that part of him, except Reya. In those Moments he was saddened that he didn't know or meet her. Only through her notebook did he get a sense of her.

After their lunches, Laura would drive back to the university and work the rest of the day and sometimes through the night on her reports. All her coworkers noticed and committed to her renewed sense of energy and focus. They often asked her to share her findings with them. Laura felt it, too. She felt alive inside for the first time in a long while, purposeful and driven to learn as much as possible from Terve and his farm.

The farm was expanding her sense of discovery and she couldn't for the life of her understand how. She began to see a correlation between her experience and some of the blog posts she read. She didn't hear wind chimes, but she could relate to being unable to sleep. She looked in the mirror most mornings expecting to see a haggard version of herself suffering from lack of sleep, but instead, she looked refreshed. Younger, even. None of it made sense and thus challenged her logical brain to the point of explosion.

Besides her sense of discovery, she found that she could see more clearly the parameters of the breakdown in the ecosystems. *Report #5115* was a launching pad that inspired several other studies. Laura applied for five other grants in her field. One of them was directly linked to the flowers that appeared arbitrarily in the fields. She hypothesized that the plants were intentionally attracted to the crops to protect them. She believed the ecosystem was trying to heal itself; that nature was attempting to defend itself against the damage inflicted upon it by humans. This particular report she knew might be controversial, but she was willing to consider the possibility. One of her colleagues, Dr. Bury, visited the farm to collect seeds to place in the global seed vault in the Arctic. The vault is a reminder of how fragile the ecosystem can be, and that the extinction of plant species is real. Dr. Bury was curious about any plant showing signs of adaptation, particularly if the adaptation supports the preservation of the species.

Dr. Bury left the farm animated and enthusiastic about the tender creatures living in the Greenhouse. She shared with Laura that a sense of hopefulness swept over her during the visit.

"I know it may sound naïve, but I don't feel so afraid about our future anymore," she told Laura. Dr. Bury wanted to enjoy the hopeful sensation for as long as she could.

Terve found himself drawn closer to Laura and felt disappointed each time she packed up and left for the day. He wanted to spend more time with her, but her focus and dedication were unwavering. When they had lunch together, she spent most of the time talking about her work and what she discovered that day. Terve found himself frustrated and a little jealous of the farm and the Greenhouse. He also felt a bit insecure. She didn't seem to be as excited about him as she was about the farm and the plants!

Terve sat at the dinner table alone. The twins are grown, and both are at different universities. Kaia comes home on the weekends, still helping Sarah with the hives. Kali's school was too far away for brief visits. There are only a handful of great veterinarian schools in the country and none of them were close to home. Terve hired someone to manage the stables. He tends to Rohkea himself but lets his employees manage the rest.

Nights are harder for him. He misses the twin's energy filling his home with life and laughter. He didn't expect their absence to hit him so hard. He had hoped that Laura and he might move closer, but she had not given him any indication of anything more than friendship between them. He wondered if, when she finished her report, he would see her as often. Even the thought of it made him tense and longing. He needed to get out of the house for a bit so he decided that in the morning he would ride Rohkea out to see Aiti. Rohkea could use a long ride and he too needed to feel nature against his skin. In the morning he'd text Laura that he was riding first thing and that he would try to make it back by lunch.

Terve finished the bourbon he was babysitting and walked upstairs to turn in early. He knew he might not sleep right away, but decided his big house felt too big for him alone in it today. He wanted the security and comfort of his room.

Dreaming:

Terve walks out the front door and looks toward the field. Reya is burying seeds in the ground but she is doing it in his fields, not the meadow. She is crying just like before but also, she is looking at the sky this time. He can't hear her. She is raising her hands and making signs with her fingers. He wants to run to her. Terve feels the desire to hold her, to be close to her. He wants to kiss Reya. He is shocked by this in his dream but continues to try to get to her. Her hands are moving in a way unfamiliar to him. She raises her hands to the sky and speaks something out loud. He still cannot hear her.

Each step he takes, he slips deeper into the earth. The soil smells putrid and he doesn't want it touching his skin. Reya continues and as she talks, the ground below her feet starts to cave in. Patches of earth start separating from the ground, but she is not distracted. Terve is fearful for her. He tries to call out for her to watch out. It feels like the earth is giving way around him.

The smell of sulfur fills his head, and he can't escape it. He tries to hold his breath while watching Reya. Seeds along with individual particles of soil start rising from the earth floating into the air. Each piece unique and on its own track. They are ascending vertically. Crops begin to disappear into the earth. Seeds and soil still rising, Terve watches them until he can no longer see them against the night's sky. Simultaneously, the ground below gives way completely and Reya falls through a large fault. Terve screams "NO!!!"

The screams awaken him. He is still screaming as he sits up in bed.

CHAPTER 21
FULL CIRCLE (FROM THE BEGINNING)

Terve and Rohkea trot toward the forest. Riding Rohkea always gives Terve a sense of freedom. The vantage point available when riding Rohkea shifts his perspective, giving way to introspection and nostalgia. He feels his presence when his arms tingle approaching the Aspens. Today, however, Terve is deep inside himself thinking about life, Laura, his children, and what will become of the farm when he is gone. The twins don't want it, although they both love it and enjoyed growing up there. They have their paths in the world and he must let go of the romantic idea that they will inherit the legacy and the mystery of this space. Terve passes Veli without noticing nor does he notice the absence of the usual birds and butterflies that greet him. He instead is feeling sorry for himself.

Rohkea senses the shift and hesitates before approaching Aiti. Terve feels Rohkea pause and looks up to see why. The forest is fuller and thick with trees. The canopy feels lower and the air thicker with a heavy stale scent lingering. Normally, this close to Aiti, his arms would be lighting up; instead, they are static along with the air. Rohkea sways side to side nervously.

Terve, sensing the horse's anxiety, touches Rohkea's shoulder and tries to calm him.

Terve dismounts and stands closer to him inching forward toward Aiti. He pushes a branch out of his view as he walks. He is shocked by the thick foliage and how difficult it is to see. Struggling a little, he stubs his foot. It's a rock from the circle. Grasping that he has arrived; he releases the reins and tells Rohkea to relax. As he looks up from the rock, he realizes that Aiti is gone along with the trees he planted for his wife. The entire circle is grown over. The only sign that it was ever there is the remaining large rocks. The comprehension that it is all gone is traumatizing. He wants to break down and cry but Terve has no tears. He is angry that Aiti, too, has abandoned him. His entire life is changing, and he is caught surprised by it somehow. As if the children would never grow up.

As if he would never get old.

As if he would never recover from losing his wife.

As if the question "What next?" would never come.

Now when he wanted to feel grounded and safe in the one sanctuary that he created, he can't. It is gone along with the veil that clouded his eyes. Indications of change were there; he just chose to ignore them.

Terve kicks the rock closest to him. "How could you Aiti?"

He is certain he broke his toe but doesn't care and kicks the rock again just to feel the pain grub deeper inside his body. He embraces the anger and the sadness together and wants to break something to soothe whatever is breaking inside him. Limping, toe throbbing, he hobbles to sit down on the rock he just kicked. Rohkea moves closer to him, sensing he needs comfort. Terve spends the next two hours without saying one word. He just looks at the space that once held asylum for him. A panic comes over him and he jumps up forgetting his foot. Pain searing, he falls to the ground and crawls. He feverishly starts moving leaves and limbs and dirt.

"Where is it? Please, let it be here!"

Terve is terrified that he won't find it. Suddenly he feels metal edges and exhales. He pushes the dirt and debris aside to find the placard he placed so many years ago. The sight of it melts the anger and frustration he carried in with him. He lays on the ground next to the placard and does something he hasn't done in a couple of years. Talks to his dead wife. Terve falls asleep, waking to Rohkea nudging him. It is getting dark. Terve looks at his watch and notices that he missed lunch with Laura. He also forgets about his foot as he jumps to his feet. The pain efficiently reminds him. He braces himself for the pain he knows he'll endure getting on Rohkea. Inhaling as he unconsciously bites down and pulls himself up, then exhaling with a few expletives, he signals Rohkea to get him home quickly.

Terve puts his best friend in his stall, feeds him, and freshens his water all while limping and grunting. When he finally gets inside, he hobbles to the refrigerator for a beer, the freezer for some ice, then makes his way to the couch to take a look at the damage he did to his foot.

He grabs his cell phone that he left on the table and sees a few missed calls from Laura. She must have given up after 2 pm but tried once more with a text around 3.

Hope you're enjoying your ride.

Missed you at lunch.

See you tomorrow.

Terve responds, not wanting her to worry, but also skillfully so that she doesn't call. He doesn't feel like talking or sharing his day with her or anyone.

Sorry.

Got caught up riding.

Talk tomorrow.

He puts the phone down and leans his head back, patiently waiting for the relief only the ice pack resting on his foot can provide.

Ice pack melted, Terve exhausted, he limps up the floating stairs. Before he closes his eyes, he takes two ibuprofen and lays in bed wondering what happened out there. How do trees just disappear? There was no indication they were removed or killed by lightning or insects. It is as if they were never there.

The next morning, he moves slowly downstairs, his foot still swollen and sore. Dark blue and purplish discolorations creep from his big toe toward his ankle. He opts for open-toed shoes for now. He decides to work in the office and do financials and process some vendor orders. In between crunching numbers and confirming supplies, he drifts back to yesterday.

Perplexed, but also emotionally raw, he walks himself through the anger and frustration he felt. With introspection, Terve finds himself in a vulnerable state. He hadn't taken time to inventory his feelings and how all the changes around him were affecting him. He must have swallowed the emotions for a long time. He was headed for one of life's transitions, and he had no control over it. He wanted to pump the brakes, but he couldn't and there lay his frustration.

"Focus, Terve," he tells himself, but instead replays his dream of Reya. Seeing her again brought up unexpected sensations that were just hanging out there. He felt exposed but confused, too. How could he feel so hungry for a person he never met? He wanted her in that Moment and felt a huge hole watching her disappear into the Unknown. Why were the seeds and soil ascending? The sulfur smell was a mystery, too, and he wished he could go back inside the dream and replay it. This time, of course, he would save Reya and they would be together.

"Well, you have really gone and lost it now man."

Lost in desire and confusion, a knock at the door brings him back. He stumbles to jump to his feet, awakening the pain just enough to focus him. He walks to the door and sees Laura standing outside. For a brief Moment, he wonders if he is just transferring his sexual frustration for Laura onto Reya. He wonders if perhaps she has come to give a signal that she is interested in him romantically. He waves her in. She just wanted to check on him and find out if they were on for lunch. Feeling too raw, Terve tells her he is caught up in the office today but would take a raincheck.

Sensing something is off about his response, Laura hesitates before accepting his answer. Terve stands still and places all his weight on one leg long enough for her to come and go. He didn't want to explain yesterday to her nor how he injured himself. Before she left, she tells him that she wants to go over some other grant ideas she has involving the farm, but it requires his approval before she can move forward.

He looks at her wishing their conversation weren't about grants at all. He fantasized about how her inquiries might be about something more seductive. For the first time, Terve could see the truth about their connection. She spoke to him as a friend, a very dear friend and someone she is forever grateful to, but Terve didn't see flirtation or foreplay in her eyes. He saw focus and work and he was merely a catalyst. His ego would have to face what his heart had already discovered.

"Not a problem, just bring me what you need me to review. If you have it with you, we can look at it later today. I will probably be in the office today doing busy work."

"Is everything all right?"

"Sure, just focused on work."

Terve tightens his jaw. Laura feels the distance between them. She feels an icy look hit her right in the face, but she doesn't understand why. She decides he looks tired and probably just needs a good night's sleep.

"Ok, then I'm off to the Greenhouse. I will see you later with the paperwork."

He waits for the door to close before limping back to his office.

Terve decides that although uncomfortable, anger is great

fuel for productivity. He puts all that intensity into his keyboard and desk, then realizes it's 4:30 pm and he hasn't eaten all day. He grills a buffalo burger with fresh tomatoes and mozzarella cheese. He grabs kettle chips and a beer and sits on a barstool in the kitchen. He glances back at the empty dinner table and feels his loneliness rising again to the surface. Heartbeat increasing, he feels throbbing in his foot. Sitting at his desk all day aggravated it. He tried to prop it up while he was working but found it too difficult to focus and type, so he put it back down. A choice he is currently regretting as he opens the freezer and grabs the ice pack again. Terve's cell phone buzzes. It's Laura's text.

Had to go to the university. If possible, can you meet me there tomorrow to go over the paperwork? 😊

Laura paused before she pushed "send." She felt it best they meet officially since she was asking him to approve future studies involving his farm. Plus, she still felt weird from their earlier conversation.

Terve read Laura's text and raised his hand to throw his cell phone, stopping only because his foot hurt too much to recover it. Her text, although totally official and without any malice, was the final straw in the past 24 hours. Terve switched from beer to bourbon and finished half the bottle. Drunk, snoring, and oblivious to the melted ice pack, he doesn't dream, he doesn't feel, and he doesn't need to because he's passed out.

A painful piercing light wakes Terve the next morning. Head pounding, tongue tasting like old garbage smells, wrapped in a cotton ball lodged in his throat. He squints to look at the clock and realizes he has overslept. Shocked, he jumps out of bed and then feels a quick reminder of last night. His foot is on fire while bile rises in his throat. He's hungover. His pores broadcast just how much he drank and how desperately he needs a shower. The stale stench of liquor rises toward his nose and he rushes to greet the toilet face first. Terve is disappointed in himself so decides he'll have a serious talk with himself later.

Terve looks long and hard at himself in the mirror, behind the swollen eyes and dark circles the golden rings surrounding his iris flicker while he speaks, acknowledging the message received.

"Ok, that's it. You had your temper tantrum and now it's time to move on. You must face your future head-on and forget the past few days. Be grateful for what you have here. No one else experiences the farm the way you do. Treasure that. Treasure your life."

Terve puts his brush down and walks away, dressing for the day. He heads downstairs sore and nauseous but ready to move forward. He will call Laura and find out what time she needs him at the university.

As Terve drives to Laura's office he makes a decision that surprises him but also makes sense. He decides to put the farm in a trust. The farm, upon his passing, will go to the university for a future scientist to study. Of course, there will be conditions. The house will remain in the family for his children. The Greenhouse must continue to grow and preserve Reya's seeds and the stables will be for Kali. Perhaps they'll use it as a vacation home and teach their children about the mysteries of the farm and the wonderous bees. Miles away from his community, Terve sees a subtle shift in the scenery. The wild grassy fields and lands look dry and dull. He gets the same feeling he had while dreaming about Reya.

Some farms look abandoned almost. Is it possible that the land changed so drastically in such a short time? Terve doesn't want to believe it but there is observable proof to suggest otherwise.

When he arrives at the university, he feels different than the first time he visited. He feels resigned. He walks into Laura's office and sits down. She grabs five binders and shows him her desire for each grant and what she'd like to accomplish. If successful and she attains all five, she will spend the next several years at the farm working alongside other scientists. Terve nods and looks at the work as she explains it. There is a proposal that explores plant evolution that catches his eye. He instantly thinks of the Greenhouse. Another proposal looks at hive collapse and potential risks to agriculture. Terve attends to Laura's words but doesn't ask any questions. When she is finished, she looks at him to see if he has anything to add.

"Yes, I do. I support your proposals, Laura, with the caveat that they do not interfere with day-to-day operations on the farm and that no harm comes to any of the crops or the hives as a result. Furthermore, I've decided to have our family lawyer draw up papers to put the farm in a trust. If anything should happen to me, I want the space preserved. I decided the best way to ensure it is to leave it to the university's science department, specifically botany. There will be exclusions and conditions that I will layout in writing so there is no ambiguity. I want the farm to be my legacy and my contribution to evolving our understanding of plants, nature, and our way of living."

Laura sits quietly, caught off-guard by his remarks that are sterile and direct but not hasty. She knows Terve means every word and all she can do is thank him. Terve signs the documents she laid out in front of him in silence and only makes eye contact when necessary. After he signs the last document, he stands up, extends his hand to shake hers, and tells her he has to get back to the farm.

"Are you sure? We could grab a cup of coffee in the cafeteria if you'd like."

"I can't today. I saw the land and some of the deterioration driving in this morning and don't want to waste a second. I need now more than ever to ensure the farm is healthy and thriving so there is a farm to leave the university."

She looks at him with empathy understanding what this means for him. She gives him his space.

"See you later then?"

"Yep."

Terve walks out her office and hesitates by the picture on the wall, expecting to run into the little girl with her father, but there is no girl and there is no response today from the picture and Terve knows he will never enter this building again.

"Time to go home," he whispers to himself. Head high, gait steady, Terve walks out of the Margret Eastwood building for the last time.

Over the years, several surveys are completed, and studies published about the farm. Laura, after finishing her work left to go on tour and brief other botanists worldwide about her findings. She began a colloquium for botanists and growers from around the world to share findings about oxidative stress and in-depth research about causes. How insects with an emphasis on honeybees and solitary bees, are impacted by the loss of biodiversity. Most of all the subtle shifts in plants observed by her and her colleagues. Laura found signs of plant's intelligence that even now she is still trying to decipher. The cellular make-up of Reya's plants were ever so slightly different than their counterparts. Lavender was still lavender but also different. She referred to it as Lavender Plus.

Terve in his own right had become somewhat of a celebrity. With the help of Kaia, he made YouTube videos about signing to plants. Some farmers and gardeners said his videos saved their crops but also brought them closer to nature. He had a large following of people who swore that Reya's seeds contained special powers. He knew the seeds were special, but even with all of the scientific data Laura produced he still felt deep down inside that there was something else yet to be discovered. He held classes regularly at the farm and persisted as a conduit connecting his community with nature.

Terve's life was full, just not in the way he had imagined. This past year, inspired by Terve's blog, an agent approached him about writing a book about his life. So, while Laura traveled the world trying to wake up scientists to the significant botanical changes and the severe impending impacts on future generations, Terve was sitting in bookstores signing autographs on the book that bore his name. He entitled the book *The Farm and The Mysterious Seeds*. Terve always included Reya in his work because ultimately, he felt she impacted his farm the most, leaving him the most precious of gifts: her notes and seeds.

CHAPTER 22
GLIMPSE INTO THE UNKNOWN

Orange rust-colored caverns
Hollow space
Walls appear smooth but textured like stucco
Endless openings to endless destinations
Seafoam green with teal highlights colored water flows through the
cavern
The water surface calm with consistent forward motion
The water never stops
The destination never realized
New caverns
New openings

CHAPTER 23
TULEVAISUUS SNEEZES

Home from signing autographs, Terve checks in on Rohkea. They don't take long rides anymore, but they spend every morning walking the farm. Terve still keeps carrots in his back pocket for him although he rarely eats a whole one anymore. Terve instead breaks them apart. Rohkea's eyes mirror Terve's, both older and weathered. Farming is a hard life and not for the faint of heart but rewarding as well. Terve knows now, with the gift of hindsight, that his life turned out just fine. When he purchased this property so many years ago, he never imagined the pure joy and expansion his heart could feel. Nor did he understand how every day he experienced new things that he could not explain or articulate to others, the tattoos, his connections to the Unknown, and the glorious mystery that he wakes up to. Terve pushes his head toward Rohkea's and leans into his dear, dear friend.

VIIME DECIDES HE IS BORED AND PULLS AT LASNA'S HEAD. TULE-
VAISUUS LOOKS UP HAPPY TO WITNESS THE ACTION. THEY BOTH
SCUFFLE AND FALL DOWN LAUGHING.

Terve feels tremors in the ground and looks up. He secures
Rohkea and walks out of the stable. The tremors come and go
quickly, long enough to shift Terve's equilibrium. He walks
slowly to the Greenhouse to check the water levels and see if
any adjustments are needed. As he steps to the threshold,
another tremor shakes the ground. This one stronger than the
last. Terve falls forward into the doorway and catches the door
as he falls. The weight of his body pushes it closed as he
stands up.

LASNA JUMPS BACK AND WRESTLES VIIME TO THE GROUND AND
TICKLES HIM; BOTH STOMPING ON EACH OTHER AS THEY PLAY.
TULEVAISUUS STARTS SHOUTING AT THEM, TRYING TO INCITE
THEM MORE.

Terve gets his bearings and looks for any signs of damage but is
distracted by a loud cracking sound. He decides to make a run
for the house. He is frightened that the Greenhouse is not safe
from whatever is happening outside, but he wants to save the
precious space from harm. Before he leaves, his hands awaken
and begin scribing symbols in the dirt and the air around the
walls of the Greenhouse. He dips his hand in water that
surrounds a few flowers and scribes faster. The earth below him
is shaking harder now, and he knows he needs to go. He takes a

step to the door but the intensity of the shaking forces him outside. He looks toward the mountains and sees a thin plume of ash or smoke coming up from the mountains.

"What the hell!!!"

Time slows as Terve watches the horizon crack along with parts of the farm. The land is separating just like his dream and the air is filled with dirt, ash and seeds. He smells the sulfur and runs toward the house.

LASNA LANDS ON TOP OF VIIME'S BACK, BUMPING HIS CHEST, CAUSING HIM TO COUGH. TULEVAISUUS STARTS TO YELL AT THEM BOTH, BUT DUST GETS IN HIS EYES AND NOSE. RUBBING HIS EYES, HE TRIES TO STOP IT, BUT IT IS TOO LATE. TULEVAISUUS SNEEZES AND FILLS THE SKY WITH ASH.

Terve struggles to walk. He feels like he is riding on a surfboard, but his legs are jelly. His legs give with each step. Inching slowly toward the porch, time stops. He hears another roar from the mountains. This time he doesn't look back. He leans in and pushes harder toward the house. Just one step short, his chest feels like a truck hit him dead on. He grabs his chest and falls to his knees. Gasping for air, he can't stop the pain writhing up his left arm, terminating at his heart. The ground disassembles and the pieces hover in midair so that the soil and the seeds appear to be dancing upward toward a floating city in the sky. Terve is lost in the magnificent destruction. Enchanted by the sight, he reaches the terrible conclusion that he is hallucinating. He falls forward, his head meets the earth, the rich ancient soil swims into the space between his teeth and he inhales the substance he will return to. Body seizing for air, his mind drifts toward his children and all that he'll miss, and Rohkea. He must check on Rohkea, but it is useless. Terve is no longer in his body but instead standing next to it, watching the life he knew leave him. He sees flickering lights in the Greenhouse and decides to investigate. The light radiating is a soft yellow, and the Greenhouse appears to expand exponentially. When he opens the door to glance inside the entire Greenhouse is filled with a crisp white light.

TULEVAISUUS LOOKS AT LASNA AND VIIME AND CHIDES THEM, ALTHOUGH SECRETLY HE ENJOYED IT. WHEN HE IS FINISHED, HE STANDS UP AND NOTICES THAT SOMETHING IS HAPPENING AT THE FARM BUT DECIDES IT IS NOT AS INTERESTING AS HE IS. TULEVAISUUS INDIFFERENTLY LAYS DOWN AND CLOSES HIS EYES.

Terve walks forward until he sees her. She is standing in front of one of her plants. She is telling it something, but he cannot hear her. He inches closer, hesitant; he doesn't want to intrude. Reya is glowing and smiling. She looks at him with familiar eyes and asks, "How did you get them to grow for you?"

"I don't think I did. I think they were just waiting for the right time, and I happened to be here."

Reya looks at Terve with deep love and kindness and extends her hand to him.

"Come on. We must tell Aiti. She will be so pleased."

Terve doesn't look back at his body lightly dusted in ash. He doesn't waiver, feeling drawn toward her. The minute he touches her hand, both of their bodies emit a soft purple aura. Terve surrenders and tells Reya.

"I'm so happy to finally meet you."

As they walk toward the Unknown, the space collapses behind them.

Terve's cell phone lay on the ground ringing; it is Kali. Missed calls from Kaia and Philip also register on the cracked screen.

Terve's body, still, unable to answer, waits to be discovered. The Greenhouse is standing and unharmed, securing each plant.

EPILOGUE

Terve's body lay along the ridgeline of a gorge that opened after he left his body. The earth welcomed him like an old friend, remembering how much love he showed it. Mounds and mounds of ash filled in the gorge, burying his body with the very richness he appreciated throughout his life. Rohkea escaped his barn, searching for Terve but was unable to find him. Frantically, he ran into the forest. Found later, laying in the space where Aiti once thrived, Rohkea succumbed.

The sneeze that started everything launched pieces of the fields in the air, carried with the wind. Kale, beets and carrots were found clumped together away from their original beds, while rows of beehives hung between the balance of earth and air waiting for the next aftershock to open the ground and seal their fate. By the time emergency responders were able to push through the damage, it was too late. Too late for Terve, Rohkea, and the bees. The Greenhouse, however, remained standing, a mystery to the first responders. Upon approach, a fireman reported a golden glow surrounding it, emanating joy. Later, they would admit that they felt guilty feeling such joy in the wake of the damage. Still standing, the Greenhouse held the love, generosity, and gifts the seeds cultivated in their keepers. Terve's home also remained, although battered. The ground beneath it, like the Greenhouse, held.

A month later, Ophelia's father is anxious to get home. They were running late because of traffic. Blocked for miles, it seemed he tried to be patient as the never-ending procession of cars turned left into a long driveway. The police escort indicated something significant was happening at the farm on the righthand side of the road. He wondered what happened and then remembered something on the news about an unusual volcanic eruption that triggered small earthquakes surrounding the property. He remembered stopping at that farm once, to pick up flowers and honey along with some organic produce at their renowned store on his way home. Ophelia, tired of sitting still, asked if she could get out and pick some of the wildflowers on the side of the road. Her father said they were weeds, but she did not wait for his approval. She opened the car door and set out to investigate the delicate purple flowers she saw. She studied each flower as a newly discovered creature. Before she picked them, she said a prayer asking where they might like to sit in her room. She waited for an answer before picking them. If an answer did not come, she moved on to the next.

Every person Terve's farm had touched came out to do what they could to help his family heal and repair. The farm store collapsed, but with some effort and creativity Sarah, Philip, and Ryan, along with many others, were able to salvage a lot of inventory. In return for the love and kindness, the twins gifted every person who attended their father's memorial with gifts from the farm store. A favorite among the items was the revered Reya's Harvest. Included in the gifts, Kaia made a custom blended shower gel to honor her father. She called it "Maailma": meaning the earth, realm, universe. Kali and Philip passed out bee hotels and asked the guests to hang them all over town as a sign of honor and respect for their father and friend. A somber occasion turned into a glorious celebration as the Greenhouse reverberated waves of sweet love and prosperity for those who attended, showering each guest with a renewed sense of being. Tears were shed, toasts were made, stories were told as a feeling of forever washed over them. Nobody wanted to leave. It felt like if even one guest stepped outside this glorious bubble, the space would dissolve, and they would all be spread to the wind.

Continued in book 3: The Apothecary
https://books2read.com/the-apothecary

GLOSSARY

Reya: Flowing, The gardener
Valo: Light, Reya's dog
Veli: Brother, Quaking aspen tree
Aiti: Mother-in-house, Mother Tree/Dragon blood tree
Kuriiri: Courier, Farmer who owns the fruit stand.
Terve: Healthy, sound, strong, Farmer and owner of the Greenhouse
Teija: gift of God, Terve's wife,
Kaia: Pure, Terve's daughter
Kali: River, Terve's son
Rohkea: Brave, Terve's horse
Nea: Flower, Terve's mother
Yli: Beyond, one of the giants/mountains
Lasna: Present, one of the giants/mountains
Viime: Past, one of the giants/mountains
Tulevaisuus: Future, one of the giants/mountains
Avaruus: Space, Pilot
Ajatella: Remember, Navigator and Avaruus' friend
Tieto: Knowledge, Co-pilot and Avaruus' friend
Sielu: Soul

Somewhere: Where Reya lives and gains the seeds.

Somewhere Else: Where Terve lives and the Greenhouse is built.

Another Place: Where Anushka lives along with the Apothecary.

Andrena: Species of bee, Apothecary employee

Colletidae: Species of bee, Apothecary employee

Apidae: Species of bee, Apothecary employee

ACKNOWLEDGMENTS

For my publisher Daniel Stombaugh at Lakeview Publishing. Your spirited guidance and positive perspective are everything. You championed me through this entire process, and I always feel supported as an artist. I wish you, the team at Lakeview and your family boundless waves of gratitude and sanctuary for your life ahead. Thank you for believing in me.

To my editor Carol Williams. The delightful sharing that erupted from working with you is priceless to me. Your kindness and tenderness were present throughout the process. As a Master Gardener you were the absolute right person to take this excursion with me.

To Bobby Barnhill, cover illustrator, thanks for your patience and wisdom beyond my recognition of what was possible for this cover. You are a professional and a gift. I am grateful for your light.

To Elizabeth Buck who gave me and Rembrandt a place to create this story when I had nowhere else to go. Thank you for your comfort and your endless giving heart and spirit.

Finally, I must again recognize the mysteries that sit in front of us all waiting patiently for us to wake up. For the tenderness that is available to all of us when we connect and tune in to nature, life and the existence of things beyond our understanding.

ALSO BY SONYA YOUNG

Folding Flags: https://books2read.com/folding-flags

The Gardner: https://books2read.com/the-gardner
The Greenhouse: https://books2read.com/the-greenhouse
The Apothecary: https://books2read.com/the-apothecary

Follow her author journey at: https://books2read.com/ap/8ZjMQj/
Sonya-Young

ABOUT THE AUTHOR

Sonya Young, author of **Folding Flags** is a veteran, artist and a nature enthusiast. After serving 20 plus years of military service and completing her MS from the University of San Diego, she turned her focus toward the artist within. Her inspiration for this book is rooted in her desire to share her experiences with nature and how it unfolds in the most unexpected ways. A resident of Las Vegas, she has spent countless hours hiking where she confesses her heart and mind feel connected totally to life.

Connect with her on Instagram or Facebook. View her visual art via her website www.artbysonyayoung.com

facebook.com/SY2021Author

instagram.com/artbysonyayoung

Made in the USA
Columbia, SC
18 September 2021